"Tell me about the best sex you ever had."

Jack's voice was low, intimate even in the large studio, soothing against the click of his camera's shutter.

Samantha closed her eyes, trying to forget she was naked under the sheet. *Click.* "I met this guy at a bar, in college. And he took me to bed. It was the boldest thing I've ever done." *Click.*

She heard Jack's footsteps coming closer. "I'm going to move the sheet."

He pulled the sheet down off her left shoulder, exposing her breast. The fabric bunched and teased between her legs, a cool, smooth bare weight like a feathery lover's kiss, leaving a fierce ache. She had to remind herself to hold still. *Click.*

Jack was still standing close; she could feel the warmth of him against her skin. "Did he make you come?"

"Ohhh, yes." She heard him curse softly. Jack slid the sheet off her other breast, this time allowing his hand to follow so his fingers trailed over her, brushing her nipple. She shivered and arched toward him.

"So it was perfect, emotionless sex." Jack's words came out husky. "And that's what you want from me? All I can say is, you can't protect yourself from the unexpected."

Samantha opened her eyes to his smoldering gaze. "I'll take that risk."

Dear Reader,

One day I was talking to a friend who said, "Wouldn't it be weird if you kept getting 'wrong number' messages on your answering machine and it turned out someone was leaving them for you on purpose?"

My writer's brain snapped instantly to attention. Why any one comment taken out of thousands of statements can be such a trigger I haven't a clue, but immediately I knew there was a book in there. So here it is! The third in the MEN TO DO series. Alison Kent, Jo Leigh and I have had so much fun coordinating our heroines, Erin, Tess and Samantha, and their stories. And if you want more, check out www.mentodo.com!

I love to hear from readers, so if you'd like to write me, please do at www.IsabelSharpe.com.

Cheers,

Isabel Sharpe

Books by Isabel Sharpe

A TASTE OF FANTASY

Isabel Sharpe

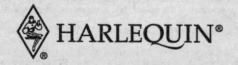

HARLEQUIN®

TORONTO • NEW YORK • LONDON
AMSTERDAM • PARIS • SYDNEY • HAMBURG
STOCKHOLM • ATHENS • TOKYO • MILAN • MADRID
PRAGUE • WARSAW • BUDAPEST • AUCKLAND

To Johnny Orion

ISBN 0-373-79080-5

A TASTE OF FANTASY

1

From: Samantha Tyler
Sent: Thursday
To: Erin Thatcher; Tess Norton
Subject: Love

What I can't seem to get my brain to stop obsessing over is: How do you know when love is real? I was so sure it was real with Brendan. Zero doubts. Zero cold feet. I stood at the altar and did the Death Do Us Part thing with my heart so full I'm surprised it didn't pop out of my grandma's dress.

If something that good and that right and that perfect, that I believed in it with every ounce of my naive-assed twenty-something passion, could turn out to be nothing more than neurotic unfounded fantasy, how do you know when it's real?

That's why I'm thinking this Men To Do thing might be the way to go right now. I'm not ready for love. Not until I can get my head around this question and get some kind of answer that makes sense.

But I sure as hell could use some sex.

Samantha

SAMANTHA TYLER INCHED THE Chevy Trailblazer into her Lincoln Park bungalow's garage. Roughly one millimeter to spare on either side or risk scratching the paint. Obviously the garage hadn't been built to accommodate ludicrously oversized vehicles. But Brendan had insisted they buy the monster, insisted they'd need it when the kids they never had were born. Brendan knew it would be so convenient for all those lovely romantic excursions they never took.

Brendan had tripped over himself leaving it to her in the divorce settlement and had immediately gone out to buy a black Audi TT Roadster to salve his feelings of rejection and failure, not to mention to attract babes. As soon as she had time she'd sell this monster and buy herself a sunshiny yellow Volkswagen Beetle. A chick car, not a Sensible Family Vehicle. As soon as she had time.

She hit the brakes and yanked the gear into park, jerked out the keys and grabbed her briefcase. Opened the door carefully so as not to hit the garage wall, and eased and squeezed her body out the half opening and into the humid August-in-Illinois air. Definitely a Volkswagen.

The garage door let out the usual series of protesting groans on its way down, followed by a final resting thud, to accompany her walk through the overgrown garden bordering the postage-stamp-sized lawn. Weeding. Trimming. Fertilizing. Mowing. Everything she saw represented something to do. As if her supposedly safe home environment was nothing but a series of tasks she was failing at.

Life had always been a joyous battle to be fought and won, or at least wrestled into temporary submission. Today life was overwhelming. She had to stuff her emotions into a bank vault or risk collapse. And she was just plain sick of crying.

Samantha jammed her key into the house lock, twisted, turned the handle, twisted again and was in. Blanche and Fudge, her black and white cats immediately came to greet her, mouths open in accusing meows. *Feed us now.*

Not cats. Tasks. How had life gotten so mundane? So colorless? So lacking in spark and love? How had she become this cold robotic nightmare of a person? So afraid to feel. But then of course she'd been that way married, too. At least now she had hope of change ahead. She could focus on that.

''My day was fine, thanks, guys.''

Briefcase on the table, shoes kicked off into the corner, rummage for the can opener, dump the food in their bowls, fresh water, a frozen entrée for herself.

The microwave started its impersonal, indifferent hum. Not like the oven, which warmed the food, coddled and cared for it, released gentle smells that permeated the house like love. The microwave heated. Heated ingredients someone wearing a hair net had slopped into nonbiodegradable plastic.

She crossed to her briefcase to check her cell phone, frowning at the grimy traces on the kitchen floor. They should invent linoleum with brown spots and dried-on pieces of lettuce in the pattern. A cleaning lady would probably be worth the money, but

Samantha hated the idea of strangers in her house, among her things.

The cell display announced that she had two messages. She stuck the phone to her ear, crossed back to the refrigerator and grabbed a bottle of Chicago-brewed Honker's Ale out of her refrigerator.

"Hi, it's Mom. Call us, we want to know how you are."

Samantha rolled her eyes. Mom wanted to make sure Samantha was miserable so she could point out once again what a mistake Samantha had made. *She'd* stayed with Samantha's father through some pretty rough times and what made Samantha think marriage was all roses and poetry and passion anyway?

A sip from the bottle, then a longer one. She didn't think marriage was all roses and poetry and passion. But it should be *some* roses and *some* poetry and *some* passion at least *some* of the time. No roses and no poetry and no passion day after day, week after week, year after year, and you might as well be living with your brother.

Next message. "Hello."

Samantha wrinkled her forehead at the throaty, unfamiliar female voice and touched the gold necklace Brendan had given her for their one-year anniversary.

"You were unbelievable last night, Johnny Orion."

Samantha's forehead unwrinkled; she rolled her eyes again. Not *another* one.

"Oh, Johnny, I didn't think my body could do all those things. Especially that many times. I can't stop thinking about you. I want to do it all again. I'm wearing black stockings and black high heels, the way I was dressed last night. I'm crazy all over again— I'm so hot for you. I'm touching myself. My hand is sliding down between my—''

Ew.

Samantha pressed the code to fast-forward the message to the end. She really should put a personal greeting on her voice mail instead of the robot announcement of her number, so these women would know she was not Johnny Orion, whoever he was. But for some reason she wanted to feel anonymous, so that even her closest friends couldn't really be sure they'd reached Samantha Tyler. She was just a number. Protected. Impenetrable. Seven digits with a hyphen in her middle.

The microwave beeped obnoxiously, announcing that it was time to ''stir contents.'' She deleted the message, the second one left in as many days for this Johnny Orion person. Two women and one last week, all sounding intelligent and articulate, all extolling his apparently unbelievable virtues in bed, all getting his number wrong. He must sleep with a lot of dyslexic women. Samantha didn't even want to *think* about how many others had managed to dial it right.

She dumped the steaming overcooked pasta, reformed chicken bits and pallid vegetables onto a plate, grated parmesan cheese over it, opened another beer and looked around for the paper. Something to read during meals to distract herself from how silent they were now. She'd have to go over work files later, a sexual harassment case, discrimination case, the usual mix of wronged people and greedy people. But not yet. A little unwind time first.

The food was edible, the business section of the *Chicago Tribune* interesting; her concentration shot. She'd have to do better than this if she wanted to get any work done tonight.

She put her elbows on the table, gripping the neck of the beer, and swung the bottle back and forth between her forearms. Johnny Orion. Probably a made-up name—wasn't Orion the hunter constellation? The guy sounded more like a predator than a hunter. She imagined a professional wrestling announcer introducing him. *And nooooow, Johnnyyyyyyy Predator!* Samantha grinned and took a long swig of her beer. Whoever he was, he certainly made women happy. Probably some well-hung young stud who serviced older married types.

The *Chicago Tribune* business section swished off the table and drifted like a giant falling leaf onto the floor. Samantha took her beer into the TV room which jutted like the short side of an L off the graceful sweep of the kitchen and living room. She pushed magazines aside, sat on the couch, legs curled under and sent a look of loathing to the TV—Brendan's Other Woman. They had a much more passionate relationship than she did with him.

She gave her work files a half-assed try, then when her usually ironclad willpower failed her, she picked up the book she'd been reading for the Eve's Apple reading group. The online group had been her salvation over the past two years as her marriage had finally dissolved. Except for Lyssa, loyal friend and officemate, her local friends had been so involved with her and Brendan as a couple that the divorce had been impossible to avoid. Even when they weren't talking about it, the topic buzzed all over them, like killer bees at a picnic.

The women in the online group knew only what she chose to reveal about herself. The discussions were lively and interesting, the books provocative and fun. And Erin and Tess were her lifeline to sanity sometimes. Her closest friends of the bunch had split off with her to form their own e-mail chat/reading sub-group. Last year the fun had been multiplied by Erin's idea of Men To Do.

Samantha smiled her second smile of the evening. Men To Do Before Saying I Do, inspired by an article in *Cosmo* which outlined several male "types" perfect for casual affairs, but hardly the stuff of "as long as we both shall live." The Vain Guy, The Rich Foreigner, the Dumb Jock and Samantha's personal favorite—The Swaggering Butthead.

Though the experiment so far hadn't turned out quite the way they'd planned. Erin got the surprise of her life when *her* Man To Do, Sebastian Gallo, who started out as The Scary Guy, turned out to be the love of her life. Then as if that weren't freaky enough, Tess had fallen madly in love with *her* fling, too. Dash Black, supposed to be The Playboy, but turned out he was happy to stop playing with every woman but her. What were the odds?

So far Samantha hadn't met anyone who fit the bill.

She yawned, ignoring the deep-down honest part of her that said she hadn't remotely been trying, and forced her eyes to focus on the book. *When Amber Burns* by Elizabeth Jader. About a woman in a happy though unexciting relationship faced with sexual temptation in the form of another man. Samantha read until her eyes and limbs were heavy and begging for sleep, her body too tired even to become aroused by the sensual words. No bed yet. Not until she was so exhausted she'd slip off immediately. Nighttime was the hardest, alone in that dark silent bedroom.

Finally she gave in, went upstairs, brushed her teeth, got into her nightgown, slid into the bed that felt like a vast empty prairie, turned out the lights and stiffened against the usual incoming creep of lonely pain.

Amazingly, tonight it didn't come.

This was good. This was progress. Maybe divorce was survivable after all, as the self-help books claimed. Samantha punched her pillow into a more comfortable shape, took in a deep breath and sighed out her relief, let herself drift off, brain minus the anxious tumble of questions and confusions.

Moments later, her bed became a jungle of tangled vines and crawling bugs and suffocating walls of trees. Johnny Orion, well-hung young stud indeed, dark-haired, sweat-sheened, ludicrously civilized in tight jeans and spotless white shirt, hacked his way through to her, eyes glowing red like a demon wolf, burning and clearing a path which widened and melted back until the bed was again a bed, sheets smooth and welcoming. But then he changed, morphed into another stranger who came to her and lay over her. Instead of weight and sweat, this man brought cleansing lightness, relief from the sticky jungle heat and confusion of overgrown vegetation. He lifted his head from her shoulder, cupped her unresisting face and touched her mouth with his…

The instant burn of sexual passion shot her awake. She reached down feverishly, pulled her nightgown up and touched herself until she arched and moaned and came alone in the dark.

She lay back, heart decelerating, breath slowing, stunned at how quickly her body had responded to the fantasy, and burst into laughter.

Hot damn.

Samantha Tyler, twenty-nine-year-old divorced mess-of-a-person, was ready for a Man To Do.

RICK GRINDLE, aka Johnny Orion, clasped his hands behind his head, and lay back on the couch, staring at the smooth white paint on his lakeside condominium ceiling. He yawned, flexed his biceps and rubbed his head absently, liking the prickly stubble feel of his shorn hair. She was thinking about him. Right now. He could tell.

He hadn't been this taken with a woman on sight in a long time. Hadn't been this intrigued or felt he would be this challenged in a long, long time. She'd come to Eisemann, Inc.—the lawyer sent to interview the bitch accusing him of sexual harassment, Tanya Banyon. He'd been in the reception area when she walked in. Even that first glimpse had hit him like a sexual storm surge. He'd taken a seat in an empty office with a view of the glass-walled conference room where she sat, pretending to be engrossed in his work, observing and ingesting her expressions and re-actions, watching her write, listen, consult papers from a file.

Samantha Tyler. God what a sexy name. Every-thing about her was sexy. Her figure, her thick blond hair, her feminine power, her assertive body language. And sexiest of all was the sadness and hint of pain lurking in her blue eyes. That sadness gave him hope. Where there was emotional vulnerability, there was always a chance to get in.

She'd felt him watching her once, turned her head and their eyes had met. The jolt of chemistry shot straight down into his pants. He hadn't reacted, made himself glance casually down at the bare desk in front of him, the anonymous indifferent stranger.

Rick lifted his head and resettled it into his hands. But his image had been planted, at very least in her subconscious. The chemical link would remain dor-mant in her brain until they met again and he chose to bring it to life, to work it to his advantage on this case and in his quest for Samantha's...*favors.*

He grinned at the ceiling, feeling the familiar stir-ring in his groin when he thought of the thoroughly enjoyable work involved in readying a conquest. Se-ducing women was an art form, one he'd mastered over his forty-two years. But in the past year or so, the chase had gotten almost too easy. Within about ten minutes he could tell if he'd be successful or not. He'd developed a nearly unerring instinct so that he minimized rejection by avoiding women who'd be impossible to conquer. Tanya Banyon had been a totally uncharacteristic misread. But women like Samantha...seemingly invulnerable but with the gift of that chink. Those women were always the best and the sweetest to overcome, though it took careful planning and patience.

"Feeling women" he called them. The most passionate, the most adventurous. Women like Samantha, who tried to hide her strong sexuality—who probably did hide it from most people. But not from him. He could sense it in the way she walked, the graceful turn of her neck, the fullness of her mouth and the glimpse of passion in her eyes.

A mourning dove announced the hour by cooing its ghostly tune from the birdsong clock on his wall. 11:00 p.m. The bars would be full. Thinking about Samantha had made him horny. Maybe he should try to find another woman tonight. Give her Samantha's cell number again, pretending it was his own, and tell her to call whenever she wanted him.

He pictured Samantha listening to the messages, wondering who he was, shocked, half-repelled, but definitely fascinated—maybe even turned-on. A woman like her couldn't help but be fascinated. Who was this Johnny Orion? Why were so many women calling for more? Wouldn't he be the perfect Man To Do?

He chuckled, got up from the couch, crossed his

spacious book-filled, rug-strewn living room into the kitchen and opened the door of his state-of-the-art built-in refrigerator. Cold beer. Or perhaps a nice Beaujolais. Pâté. A baguette from Mon Pain. Strips of bright red pepper. No other women tonight. Tonight he'd sit here, get slowly stewed, maybe hack into her computer and see what else she revealed to her friends, or just think about her and how good it would be between them when he finally landed her.

"HOLD THAT." JACK HUNTER took a step back and eyed the models critically. The tall brunette—Yvette was it?—stood stiffly, body oiled and bronzed, hair slicked down, wearing a glittering, chest-flattening thong bikini. In front of her, on a clear plastic seat that would not show up in the shoot, back pressed firmly to the tall model's stomach, arms raised like armrests, sat another model, similarly attired. The overall effect, once the picture was done, would be of a female human piece of furniture.

Jack moved forward and carefully rearranged a wayward strand of the seated model's hair. Vanessa he thought she was called. "Good. Hold that. No emotion. Stare straight."

He moved behind the tripod set up with his Hasselblad camera, loaded with two-and-a-quarter-inch film and gazed down into the lens until the models became in the viewfinder what he wanted in his mind. Stiff. Wooden. Unemotional. Perfect. He pressed the shutter. Then again, jaw tight, adrenaline high.

Something about the way female bodies could be

molded and manipulated to resemble household objects fascinated him. The ability to represent the inanimate with the living, to merge object and life, to cross the boundaries of function and form. This project was his baby. He didn't need to do it. Commercial shoots gave him all the work he wanted. But photography for the sake of art instead of in homage to capitalism fed his soul in a way his regular job, no matter how satisfying, never could. The ultimate rebellion from pictures that glorified the mundane in order to seduce the consumer. Cereal as the next Messiah, cars that would change your life and social status, jewelry that would save your marriage.

This shoot was about simplicity, about something as complicated as a human being arranged into something as stark and serviceable as a chair. The contrast was irresistible.

He shot a few more frames, then adjusted the main light brighter, to make the shadows more harsh.

"Yvette." He raised his head and frowned at the standing model. "Can you take the light out of your eyes? Make them dead. Like you're blind, like you're seeing nothing. Can you do that?"

The model unfocused her eyes into dull blank circles.

"Excellent. Almost done." He bent his head back over his camera and snapped a few more shots, finished the roll and nodded. "Thanks. Good work."

The women slumped out of their positions with sighs of relief and rolled necks and arms stiff from posing for so long.

Jack clapped his hands in brief applause. "You ladies did great. You can get dressed now. I'll send you prints for your portfolios in a week or two."

The women made their way to the changing area at the back of his studio to shower and dress.

Jack shut off lights, labeled his rolls of film and took them to the darkroom. Good day today. He'd nailed several shots exactly as he wanted them. The women had been even better than he hoped. He could afford professional models, but he liked finding women on his own, usually aspiring models or performers who were comfortable in front of a lens already. He gave them the pictures for their portfolios or for their amusement or egos, or whatever they wanted them for, and saved himself contracts and legal hassles.

Best of all, he could go about the project leisurely, wait until he found the right faces, the right bodies for the poses he wanted.

This shoot wrapped up his chair series. His next was even more complicated—women as dining tables. Intimate feasts for two served on a woman's horizontal spine. Fabulous. Someday he'd do a whole dining set.

He put his Hasselblad away in the cabinet Dad had made for the studio. He was looking for a very special person for the table shoot. Someone who could project the kind of simple sincerity the picture required, to avoid a comic effect. Someone who could fill the frame without trying to—or even while trying *not* to. He wasn't even sure what she would look like, only that he'd know when he found her. Something about her would spark certainty that she would photograph well and transform his internal vision into reality.

The women emerged from the bathroom, hair still damp, giggling over some joke.

He threw off the focus and tension that always accompanied his work and grinned. "You ladies interested in having a drink?"

They shot each other sidelong glances that made him feel like a dirty old man. Okay, so he was probably ten years older than they were. Not like he wanted anything more than company for a drink. His big scoring days were over. But having two visions of loveliness on his arm for the evening wasn't exactly an ego buster. So shoot him, he was human.

"Come on. Do I look like a cradle robber?" He held his hands out in surrender which made the girls giggle. "I'll buy you a drink to thank you for the good work you did here."

More sidelong glances. The fluent silent communication that only the female of the species understood.

Hmm. Women didn't usually respond to his charm as if he were a walking virus. Fine. Forget it. Not like he had anything invested in their company.

"We were thinking." Yvette sidled up to him on one side and took his arm.

"Oh?" He looked down at her lovely face turned up impishly toward him and couldn't help grinning. A promising sign.

"Yes." Vanessa slid around to his other side and took his other arm. "We were thinking."

"Thinking, huh?" Jack turned to the lovely impish face on his other side and couldn't help grinning wider. "Is this unusual activity for you?"

Two sweet giggles, high and breathy, one in one ear, one in the other. Okay, so he'd been in worse situations.

"We were thinking maybe…" Vanessa tipped her head to one side and looked at him through half-closed eyes.

"Yes…?" He couldn't help feeling cocky. They were going to accept. Instead of going to his empty apartment, or going out to eat on his own, he'd have some company, maybe get some flirt. It had been a while; he'd been so intent on his work. Just some harmless fun.

"That maybe…" Yvette took up the sentence. "You'd like to do both of us."

A burst of incredulous air exited his mouth. *What?* The girls were barely out of diapers, and they were suggesting a threesome? "*Do* you?"

"Yeah." Yvonne wiggled seductively closer. "Both of us."

"Uh…" Jack swallowed. This was supposed to be every man's dream. Ten years ago—maybe even five—he'd have instantly gotten so hard his cock would have ripped through his pants.

It wasn't happening now. Instead of a hard-on, he was suffering from a sudden surge of panic. No question his attitudes about women had changed. His attitudes about a lot of things had changed.

"I'm not sure that would be such a good idea."

"Awwww." Yvette stood on tiptoes and trapped his left earlobe between her teeth.

"C'mon." Vanessa wrapped one leg around his and pressed her pelvis to his right thigh, hands clamped onto his chest. "It'd be fun."

"I'm sure it would be." Jack extracted himself from trapping teeth, clamping hands and pressing pelvis, feeling like he was stripping off too-tight clothes. "But I can't."

"Why?" Yvette backed off and crossed her arms over her chest.

"Because I don't need a reputation for hiring models and screwing them."

"Ha!" Vanessa pouted and shot him the look of a snake to its mousy prey. "You already have one."

Jack held himself still. Made long, icy eye contact first with one girl, then the other. "I think you should leave."

They glanced at each other, then grimaced and filed sulkily past him through the reception area to the old freight elevator used when the building was a warehouse.

He waited until he heard the slide and groan of the doors shutting behind them.

Crap.

Youth was like a savage wonderful drug. You thought the world could be yours. You thought you could get away with anything. You thought you could indulge your passions and whims in this glorious free-for-all called adulthood and suffer nothing. No consequences. No guilt. Out of your parents' house and into the candy store for dinner.

Jack took a quick glance around for anything out of place, turned off the studio lights and took the elevator up to his apartment. Miraculous that he hadn't made a mistake sooner. Three years ago he'd spent the night with a type of woman he usually avoided. A particularly determined woman, who wouldn't take no for an answer. Something about her aggressiveness, something about her confidence and primal no-nonsense, bad-girl sexuality had gotten to him, and he gave in to an explosive encounter.

He was still paying for it. The next morning he'd woken up, disoriented and edgy. Sleeping with models was dangerous; he knew that. Until that night he'd felt untouchable, chosen wisely, parted on good terms. But this woman had psycho written all over her and he'd gone ahead anyway, mind blunted by booze, ignoring the fact that someone like her could cause major problems for his blossoming career.

She had. For some screwed-up reason she'd decided that one night entitled her to complete ownership. When he'd rejected her next advance, politely but firmly, she'd turned on him so fast, with such violent and ugly determination, he barely had time to react.

Apparently no one rejected Krista Crotter and lived happily ever after. She made sure as many business associates of his she could get her hands on knew about what had happened. Or at least knew her version of what had happened.

He went into his living room, crossed the Oriental rug over plank flooring and put Annie Lennox's *Diva* CD on the ridiculously overpriced sound system he'd splurged on a few years before on some testosterone-laden buying spree. He hit "skip" until he found his favorite tune, about how life felt like walking on broken glass.

It had taken months and months of damage control, of walking the fine line between keeping Krista down and pissing her off more, to extricate himself from the nightmare with his reputation intact.

Fairly intact.

Jack passed his hands over his face and blew out a long breath. No question now, but he needed a drink. He opened his refrigerator, which yawned spotless and practically empty except for the orange box of baking soda. No beer. And he should probably change the baking soda, not that there were any odors in there to absorb at the moment.

The total lack of beer decided him. Even without company, he'd go out, something he rarely did anymore, especially by himself. Booze and available women were easier to avoid if he stayed home.

But tonight he felt restless here in the perfectly organized apartment that usually soothed him. What harm could it do? One beer, maybe two. And if he met a woman, he could prove to himself that he could talk to her without getting his anatomy involved.

He went into his bedroom, frowned at a piece of

paper that must have blown off his desk, replaced it and closed the window to the offending night air. Humming along to Annie Lennox, he changed into tan linen pants and a white cotton shirt with a beige stripe and descended to the underground parking area he had built for his staff, clients, and other tenants in the converted industrial building he'd bought five years previous with a loan from Dad. A loan he was well on his way to repaying, even after the damage Krista tried to inflict on his career.

He climbed into his Camry and headed east on Division toward State Street, enjoying the soft air through his rolled-down windows, sweet and summery in spite of the city noise and bustle. Weird sexual invitation aside, he was glad now that Tweedle-gorgeous and Tweedle-more-gorgeous hadn't accepted his invitation to come out tonight.

It felt good to be alone.

2

From: Erin Thatcher
Sent: Thursday
To: Samantha Tyler; Tess Norton
Subject: re: Love

How do you know when love is real? Is that the question of our generation or what? A year ago I'm not sure I could've given you an answer, Sam. I'm still not sure I can tell you anything you don't already know. As amazing as things are with Sebastian, I'm still no expert on love and relationships.

For what it's worth, though, here goes.

The thing with Brendan wasn't all right and perfect or you would still be with the bastard. I guess all I can say is that it takes two people to make it real and maybe, from this distance now of several months, you can look back over the last few years and see where Brendan may not have been on board for the long haul. Or where he may have taken a different fork in the road halfway through the journey. I never knew him. I only know what you've told us about him.

Just don't let this one failure turn you off men or relationships. Because it was not your failure. It was his.

Love you! Erin

From: Tess Norton
Sent: Friday
To: Samantha Tyler; Erin Thatcher
Subject: re: Love

Sex is good. Sex is fun. In fact, I think instead of an apple a day, doctors should prescribe a lay a day. However, sex is not love. Now that I think about it, I think there should be two different words for sex...one when you're in love, and one where you're not. Both of which would be positive, affirming, with no derogatory elements.

Sex (the one without love) and perhaps Slovex (the one with). Hmm. I gotta work on that.

As for the whole question of how you know love is real...um, gosh. That's tough. Because it's totally experiential, and not at all objective. (Am I helpful or what?) I think I fell in love with Dash that first night out. Something shifted inside, and it had nothing to do with sex, and everything to do with sex. I was hit by Cupid's arrow, I guess, which makes as much sense as any other theory. The thing is, there's no way to know if it's everlasting love unless you go through everlasting. Or read the *Cosmo* love horoscopes. I'm not sure which. <g>

Trust your heart. Trust your instincts. Give yourself

permission to love freely, and accept love in return. In the meantime, go get laid.

Love, Tess

SAMANTHA HUNG UP the phone and frowned, swiveling back and forth in her office chair, tapping a pen to the side of her cheek. Another sexual harassment case. On the one hand, the accuser, Tanya Banyon, admittedly a rather...*obvious* sort of female. On the other hand, Rick Grindle, the accused. Samantha had only gotten a glimpse when she visited Eisemann, Inc. but by all accounts, including the one she'd just gotten from a female colleague of his, he was charming, intelligent and thoroughly professional.

Usually in these cases it was only a matter of a few interviews before Samantha could tell either of two things. One, that there had simply been misunderstood personal boundaries and communications, or two, one party was lying. Rick Grindle had been unavailable for a personal interview so far. She'd go that route next.

"What's doing?" Her assistant, Lyssa, poked her head into Samantha's office.

Samantha shrugged. "Just wrapping up before I go home."

Lyssa pushed the door open with her shoulder and marched in, carrying an armful of files which she dumped onto Samantha's desk. "I come bearing gifts."

"Oh, joy." Samantha gave her a wry grin. Lyssa was tall, blond and curvaceous. She exuded a fresh sweet sexual quality that had men hurling themselves after her as she walked down the street. The kind of woman who made any other woman near her feel old and stale, like recycled airplane air. If Lyssa wasn't a genuinely grounded, warm person, Samantha would hate her.

"Anything exciting on the agenda tonight?"

Samantha lifted an eyebrow. "Is there ever?"

Lyssa smiled, showing, of course, perfect white teeth—a smile Samantha had seen reduce cold, cocky vice presidents to blushing beings from Planet Idiot. "You could change that, you know."

"I know, I know. But I'm not—" The word "ready" got as far as the inside of her teeth before her brain stopped it. Hadn't she just decided last night that she *was* ready?

"Bill and I are going out to Excalibur tonight. Want to come along?"

Samantha hid her wince. If she was going to play third wheel, at least she'd like to play it to someone other than Bill. Lyssa had this amazing, unerring ability to fall for unattractive, selfish, annoying boy-men. "Thanks, I'm pretty tired. Long week. I think I'll finish here and go home. Maybe another time."

"Suit yourself. But I think it's high time you started bestowing that gorgeous bod on deserving men again."

Samantha rolled her eyes. "I'll take that under advisement."

Lyssa laughed. "Okay, so I'm intruding. You need anything else before I go?"

"No, no." Samantha waved her off. "Go have fun, eat chicken wings, drink, go deaf. Enjoy it."

She watched Lyssa leave the room, ready to go out and have a ball on a Friday night, even if it was with a selfish, annoying boy—man. While Samantha would go home, dump her briefcase on the already cluttered dining room table, feed the cats, eat bad food and end the evening cuddled up with a book about someone else having sex.

A sudden restless rebellion swelled in her chest. She couldn't face that tonight. Closed in with her loneliness and her confusion and her cats and her work and those damn frozen dinners.

Enough. Tonight she was going out.

She turned impulsively to her computer, logged into her home account and hit "Create Mail."

From: Samantha Tyler
Sent: Friday
To: Erin Thatcher; Tess Norton
Subject: Readiness

Newsflash. I know I've been a wimp. I know I've been hanging back. I'm not even sure what changed my mind, except maybe that I had a totally hot dream last night.

But as of this date, Friday, August ninth, my Man To Do hunt has begun in earnest. Chances are I will go sit in a bar tonight and look available and pathetic, but there is always the hope that someone and something will happen that will involve nudity and sweaty writhing and many many orgasms. It's been too damn long.

I have spoken.
Samantha
P.S. I'll let you know details tomorrow.

She clicked the send button, shoved her chair back and stood, grabbing her briefcase. She wasn't usually this spontaneous, but then her life hadn't been usual in a while. It would be great to be out, surrounded by her fellow Chicagoans, noise, energy and life.

Chances she'd find someone and then actually go for it tonight were slim, but the fantasy of being with someone deliberately unsuitable was delicious. Men to Do Before Saying I Do. After a bad marriage, divorce, and all the angst that went with them, a fun-only fling was exactly what she needed. To indulge attractions for types of men she could no more get serious about than enjoy shopping for feminine protection.

And speaking of protection, she still had the condoms she'd bought on a particularly rebellious day last spring after the divorce, when she thought she was ready for a wild night.

Not.

She'd met a guy, a sweet, overly earnest type, well over six foot and solid. At the time she'd been so angry and grieving that she'd practically thrown herself at him. After two hours of beer and innuendo they'd gone outside together, ostensibly to drive to his apartment. She'd kissed him twice, burst into tears, sobbed violently for half an hour and completely freaked the poor guy out.

Okay, so divorce did not leave her at her most rational.

But that wouldn't happen this time. She was ready now. She felt peaceful and stable, rather than manic and confused. She was acting out of genuine need this time, making a strong deliberate choice, not reacting to pain and fear.

She closed her office door and strode through the building to the underground garage, calling good night to a few fellow employees. The Blazer started up; she backed it out of her reserved space and headed into the still-blazing day. She was in the mood for a fun place with a bar, but also decent food, not the packed-to-the-gills meat-market type places. P.J. Clarke's in the Gold Coast would do it.

She found a parking place in an adjacent lot and walked toward the restaurant entrance, wishing she'd gone home to change out of her business suit and into something more casual, maybe a little funky. Maybe even a little sexy. Except if nothing happened when she was in her suit, it was easier to look like she was out for a nice lone-woman dinner and to heck with everyone else. There was something sad about sitting at a bar decked out in hot-to-trot finery and striking out. A situation that would have her imagining all the other bar patrons whispering and shaking their heads.

Poor thing. Out to get some and no one biting.

She swung open the door, letting cool confidence take over her body, though she was shaky inside, half nerves, half excitement. No problem. Move forward and chant the mantra: *Samantha Tyler does this kind of thing all the time. Take me or leave me. I'm here.*

She squared her shoulders and walked with deliberate indifference toward the bar, avoiding eye contact. Her senses registered the buzz of conversation and the stink of cigarettes, the measuring eyes of guys turning to see who had walked in. The row of round-topped wooden stools mostly, but thank God not all occupied, beckoned. Her mind raced as she calculated which seat would be best. Not next to the creepy middle-aged guy. Not next to the ponytailed artsy-looking guy. *Not* next to the twenty-something sexpot girls. That comparison she could do without.

There. Three people leaving. She could sit in the middle seat and avoid choosing someone to be next to.

She ordered a draft ale and concentrated on gazing at the bottles behind the counter, keeping her expression neutral. Someone was watching her. She could feel it. A shiver of excitement went through her for no apparent reason. What was that? For some equally unapparent reason, a vision of tall, dark and hunky rose in her mind, when the eyes on her could just as easily belong to a transvestite admiring her outfit.

Who? She turned her head slightly; no one on that side. She scanned with peripheral vision behind her. Nope. But the feeling was increasing, a shivery dangerous sexual sensation. Someone was coming up to her, about to speak. She'd never sensed anyone's presence as powerfully as she did this person's.

Who?

She turned the other way.

Oh. My. God.

He was sitting two seats from her on her left; she

hadn't noticed him arriving. She *certainly* would have noticed if he'd been there when she walked in. Talk dark and hunky, uh huh. And with this sort of bad-boy Jimmy Dean quality about him, as if he'd been orphaned as a young boy and fought his way through to adulthood on grit, determination and muscle.

Okay, so maybe that was a bit much to deduce after one glance. But oh, my, he was someone she'd be happy to talk to. The only strange thing was that after meeting his eyes, that strong sense of being approached by something exciting and dangerous had faded. She felt safe again. Still excited and…very excited. But safe.

"Hi." One side of his mouth twisted up in a crooked smile, while the other side stayed emotionally neutral and seriously sexy.

She studied him, her head tilted to look as if she was deciding whether he was worth responding to, while her heartbeat was telling her in rapid and certain terms that he was.

"Hi."

He kept that sly smile on, leaned toward her and extended his hand. "I'm Jack."

She looked down at his hand, then up into his eyes before she took it. "Samantha."

His grin widened to include the other side of his mouth and he chuckled.

She raised an eyebrow. "That's funny?"

He shook his head, still smiling.

She tightened her lips, not really annoyed. The same old joke had gone beyond annoying. "I know,

I know, Samantha on *Bewitched,* and am I a witch, and if I wiggle my nose can I make you disappear?''

"Nope."

"No?" She smiled, curious, and frankly unable to keep from smiling back at him. Something about the way he looked at her made her feel strangely happy. Maybe it was just that he seemed interested, but plenty of men had been interested, and she didn't recall it necessarily involved this kind of...uplift, for lack of a better term.

His eyes were brown, lighter than dark deep endless brown, but full of life, full of male confidence and messages that he knew that she knew and that if they both wanted it to, something could happen.

This could be a really, really outstanding evening.

"I was thinking of another Samantha."

"Okay, let me guess. The character on *Sex and the City* who falls into bed with every man she meets."

He laughed and gestured forward to the seat next to her. "Is this taken?"

Samantha swung her legs back under the bar and shrugged. "Nope."

He slid off the stool and moved closer. She hadn't realized how tall he was—well over six feet—nor how imposing. And boy, did he smell good. Male and sophisticated—what was that scent? She hadn't a clue but she wanted to roll in it like a dog and smell it on her own body later.

He settled himself onto the stool next to her and smiled. "That's better."

Close up he was even more magnificent. His hair

was thick and slightly wavy, cut short so the muscles in his neck were visible when he bent his head forward. The back of men's necks and their shoulders, that powerful broad expanse, was a turn-on to her.

"Samantha."

He said her name as if he was contemplating the taste of it, sliding it around his tongue and mouth before he swallowed it and made it part of him. The sound did shivery schoolgirl things to her insides, so she kept her face rigid, since it was silly at her age to be feeling this light-headed over the sound of her name.

"Samantha was the name of a very, very special…female." He took a sip of his beer and turned to look full into her eyes, his softening as if the memory was taking him over.

Samantha narrowed hers. Something lurked in the back of those eyes. Something extremely mischievous. A very, very special…*female?*

She shook her head and turned back to her beer. "Your dog."

He burst out laughing and slapped his hand on the bar. "Damn, you're good."

She bit off the obvious line. A bit too soon to be agreeing, even playfully. She knew where *that* would lead. And even if she ended up wanting it to lead there, now was too soon to start in with the serious flirting.

He angled his body toward her and leaned one elbow on the bar. "So what do you do, Samantha?"

"I'm a lawyer."

"Corporate."

"How did you know?"

He tapped the side of his head. "I'm brilliant."

She snorted. "I'll keep that in mind."

He took a sip of beer, straight out of the bottle—Leinenkugel's Red, brewed up north in Wisconsin. Drinking out of the bottle was sexy on men. Samantha approved.

"What kind of law?"

"I'm corporate counsel for ManForce temporary agency. I handle discrimination cases mostly, racism, sexism and sexual harassment."

"Uh-oh." He held up his hands. "I better watch what I say."

She lifted her brows acknowledging his statement, but not responding. Never hurt to get that information on the table. Men were usually pretty wary after they found out what she did. Nice little weapon, one she wasn't afraid to use, not that she got herself in situations like this often. But by the way his eyes warmed at the sight of her, she was starting to be damn glad she'd gotten herself into this one.

"And what do you do for fun, Samantha?"

He spoke softly, suggestively. Samantha started to roll her eyes, but then it occurred to her that if he kept up this kind of macho pickup-line crap, he might qualify as the Swaggering Butthead and then she'd get to see him naked. "Define fun."

"Nonwork activities." He winked. "You don't strike me as the type that sits in bars for excitement."

"Oh?" For some reason that stung. As if she had

Desperate Divorcée written all over her instead of Confident Woman On the Prowl. "What type do I strike you as?"

"Beautiful, classy, elegant." He looked her over as if he was thinking about having her for dessert. "More at home at the opera, or the symphony or in a five-bedroom split level with hubby and lovely children."

She narrowed her eyes. "Are you trying to charm or insult me?"

"I'm trying to be honest. How you take it is up to you."

Samantha gritted her teeth at the same time she was starting to get seriously excited. Mind games. Just what a true Swaggering Butthead was into. Keep his prey off-balance, subjugated. "I'm not into opera, I go to the symphony maybe twice a year, no kids and…" She gave a nonchalant shrug, though it was still hard to say. "I'm not married."

"Divorced."

She shot him a look. Yup. He had her pegged. One deep to-hell-with-you breath and Samantha regained her composure. "It happens."

"You didn't think it would?"

"No. Of course not."

"Of course not." He tipped the beer back into his mouth and put it down on the bar with an emphatic thud. "If you ask my opinion, which you didn't, marriage is a fairy tale force-fed to us from birth."

He paused for her reaction. She gave him none. "It's unreasonable to expect two people to be able to stand each other's neuroses for all eternity. But there you have it every day." He gestured with his hand and let it slap onto the bar. "People standing at the altar, sure that mindless infatuation bound to deteriorate is something special and mystical and everlasting. Am I right?"

"You're right."

He looked surprised, as if he'd only been baiting her in his best Swaggering Butthead manner, and was anticipating a surefire reaction of hysterical female outrage. "You agree?"

"No. You're right, I didn't ask your opinion."

He blinked once, then clutched his chest as if she'd shot him. "You got me."

"Easy target."

"I guess." He signaled the bartender, pointed to their glasses and held up two fingers. "Can I buy you another beer?"

She rolled her eyes, secretly enjoying his high-handedness. *Swagger on, baby; you're doing just fine.* "Apparently you can."

A couple moved away from two stools behind him at the bar; a trio of thirty-something guys wedged themselves into the space. Jack Hunter slid off his stool, pulled it closer to her and slid back on, acknowledging the thanks of the men behind him.

"So." He grinned, his knee nudging the side of her thigh.

"So." She gave him an offhand look, hoping he'd think the flush on her face was from the warm bar and the beer. "What do *you* do?"

"Guess."

"Hmm." She pretended to look him over carefully, as if she hadn't been doing that already from the second they met. Nicely dressed, linen pants and a loosely woven cotton shirt. No jewelry, early thirties she'd guess. But describing his clothes didn't begin to capture his real look. The male confidence, the killer eyes that were so magnetic it looked as if they were lit from inside....

"You're a male stripper."

He burst out laughing. "Now *how* did you guess that?"

Samantha shrugged, trying to contain her own laughter. God this was fun. Beat the hell out of staying at home with Blanche and Fudge. "It's written all over you. Jack the Stripper."

He laughed again, this time letting his eyes linger on hers after the chuckles died. She held his gaze for a few seconds, then looked away. Holy heat wave. The chemistry was astounding.

"I'm a photographer. I shoot commercial stuff primarily, but I'm also working on a series for a gallery on Carpenter Street."

"No kidding."

He grinned, a slow charmer's grin that made her grab her beer for a long sip. "No kidding."

Samantha put her glass down and ran her finger around the rim, not at all mystified by her sudden need to touch. "One feeds your pocketbook, one feeds your soul?"

"Yes." His eyes shifted from lazy sex to sudden

alert focus, as if she'd surprised him by being in possession of a brain, lawyer or not. "Exactly."

"Very nice."

"I'm glad you approve." He sat watching her, drumming his fingers on the bar as if he was considering something carefully.

Samantha shot him a look. "So, have you decided?"

He cocked his head in a question. "Decided?"

"Whether to say it or not."

The same surprised awareness flickered through his eyes before he laughed and leaned his chin on his hand, looking at her like she was a piece of his very favorite chocolate cake. "Yes."

"And?"

"It's a go." He grinned, still watching her intently. "Have you ever done any modeling?"

She let one eyebrow slide halfway up her forehead, while her insides started to jitterbug. Oh. Wow. This could be it. "No."

"I think you might be right for a project I'm starting soon. Interested in doing a test?"

She let her lids lower suspiciously. "What makes me right where a professional model wouldn't be?"

"Hard to say. Call it instinct, call it artistic selection. I could easily be wrong, but I think a camera would love you. I think you have exactly what I want."

His voice was smooth and low, his eye contact direct and no-nonsense. Samantha shrugged and took another sip of her beer, which was pretty amazing considering she felt like gasping and slumping onto the bar. Wow. Unless she was totally wrong, this was the photographer's equivalent of asking her to come see his etchings. What were the odds she'd find the perfect Man To Do the very night she was finally ready? If she wasn't so cynical, she'd consider another attempt at believing in Fate.

"I see." She tipped her head to the side and pushed her hair behind one ear in a consciously seductive gesture, pleased when his eyes followed the movement. "What kind of project?"

"I'm doing a series of photographs of women as pieces of furniture."

Samantha nearly burst out laughing. Ha! What could be more Swaggering Butthead-y than that? Women as objects! He was getting better all the time. "Furniture?"

"Chairs, dining tables, that kind of thing." He grinned an I-know-what-you're-thinking grin.

"Charming. Do you seat men on them? Smoking cigars and flicking burning ashes on their skin?"

"Hmm. No." He tilted his head and rubbed his chin. "But now that you mention it..."

Samantha rolled her eyes. "Oof."

"It's a concept. It has no bearing on how I feel about women. I could just as easily use men."

"Then why don't you?"

"Because women's bodies are more interesting to me. A man's body impersonating a wooden object is less of a draw. But take the soft strength of a woman, her beauty, her living grace, and transform that into something without life, something utilitarian. That's such a clear contradiction, a clear paradox. And beautiful visually.''

"I see." She swung her legs toward him and away on the bar stool. Something about that furniture thing bothered her. And something about hearing him talk about women's bodies *really* bothered her. But in an entirely different way. One that had her wondering if his etchings might be something she'd really like to see.

"So..."

She turned toward him again. "So?"

"Are you interested?"

"In being your dining table?"

That slow grin spread itself across his face. "In coming to the studio for a test."

She knew what that meant. Knew what it would mean if she said yes. And staring into his dynamite eyes, that were sending signals she didn't need a translator to decipher, she thought maybe Jack Hunter, Swaggering Butthead extraordinaire, was exactly what she needed. "I think I might be."

"You think?"

She looked back down at her beer and hooked a finger through her necklace, moving it back and forth. Men were lucky. *Fatal Attraction* type psychofemales aside, they could generally rely on their physical power to stay safe. Women were more vulnerable. "I just don't know if you...I mean I don't know you."

He nodded. "Understood. Here's my card. The studio is on West Walton street, not too far from here."

She accepted the card and studied it. Nice address. If he was legit, he was probably doing well for himself.

"My clients include Henderson, Algram and Cairns, Stoering Medical Systems, the French designer Paul Justin and Watson Sports."

Samantha tried not to look impressed in spite of the fact that she was. Henderson, et al. was one of the biggest if not *the* biggest advertising agency in the city; Paul Justin was sweeping the nation designing everything from watches to socks, and the other two companies were just shy of the Fortune 500 list.

Of course successful people could be creeps, too, but somehow in her book it made him less likely to be into tying her up, torturing her, and dumping her into Lake Michigan. Maybe it was false security, but she liked the feeling. And he was definitely the sexiest guy she'd encountered in a long time. Or ever.

She threw him a sidelong glance, designed to get him hot and bothered, which boomeranged unexpectedly off his mega-male presence and got her hot and bothered instead.

To hell with security and common sense. When was the last time she'd encountered chemistry like this? Not since she met Brendan. Maybe not even then.

She was going to do it.

She tucked the card into her purse and smiled at him, pushing back her hair again, as if she thought it had any hope of staying behind her shoulder. "Okay."

"Okay?"

"I'll do it."

He thumped his fist on the bar and laughed as if he'd been holding in tension waiting for her answer and was finally able to let it out. "Good. I think you'll be perfect for the project. How does next week sound?"

Samantha determinedly kept the smile on her face while her stomach bottomed out. He really did want to photograph her? It wasn't just an excuse to get her alone tonight?

"Uh…"

"You should know, though—" He rubbed his chin again. "I can't do this on regular studio time or use my staff, so it would have to be kind of late. Say eight o'clock."

Samantha's determined smile started to feel more natural. "I see."

"And I should warn you ahead of time…" He quirked an eyebrow and leaned closer as if to whisper. "That the women in these pictures aren't suffering from an overabundance of clothing."

Samantha's stomach resumed its regularly scheduled functions and poured in an extra dose of adrenaline. Late evening shoot. No staff. Barely any clothes.

All was not lost.

He could still be her Man To Do. Just not tonight. Which was actually okay. Guys with true evil on their minds would be more likely to jump on her right now, not wait until a convenient time slot turned up. This way would feel a lot safer, even if it lost something in the passionate spontaneity department. And she could put in some serious fantasy time over the next week.

"I think I could handle that."

"I think you could." His grin spread extra slowly; his eyes held hers until she had to look away and fish clumsily in her purse for a business card. "Here's my work number."

"Good." He accepted her card and turned it over in his strong-looking fingers. "I'm looking forward to it."

Not even a fraction as much as she was.

"So am I." She grinned back at him and lifted her second beer in a private toast. To Samantha: on her way to moving on from Divorce Hell. To Jack Hunter: Swaggering Butthead and possible Man To Do.

She smiled as an absurd thought struck her. And to whatever and whoever he was doing tonight—Johnny Orion.

RICK DROVE HIS Jeep Cherokee into a space opposite Samantha's driveway and shifted into park. Good. She was home safely. The guy in the bar hadn't followed her. And she looked much happier than when she left. He'd driven by her house earlier in the evening, wanting to see the space she lived in, to get more of a feel of the kind of person she was, then driven to her office and followed her impulsively when he saw her come out of the garage. Then he'd followed her home—to make sure she was safe and because she enchanted him and he didn't want to break the connection until he had to.

He turned on his car radio. An obnoxious pop song came on; he frowned and changed the station to WFMT. The noble music of Bach and Beethoven was better suited to thoughts of Samantha than some prepubescent boy band.

Tonight had been good. He'd approached her at P.J.'s when she first came in and sat at the bar, not to speak to her, to let her sense him. She had. He could tell by the way her body tensed, by the way she turned her head to see behind her. She was looking for him. Wanting him without even knowing she did. Then that guy had intervened. Jack, he called himself. That was okay. Rick was nothing if not patient. He'd had competition before. It complicated things, yes, but also made them more interesting.

Lights went on in her house, indicating that she'd gotten safely inside. The overture to Wagner's *Tannhäuser* swelled on his car radio as if celebrating that fact. Rick smiled at the glowing windows, at the glimpses of Samantha moving from room to room, closing the curtains. He felt like a Peeping Tom, but if ever there was a woman worth peeping at…

I am not to speak of you—I am to think of you
When I sit alone or wake at night alone

I am to wait—I do not doubt I am to meet
you again
I am to see to it that I do not lose you.

"To a Stranger," by Walt Whitman. Maybe he
should write the poem down and send it to her. She'd
like it. But not yet. Sending notes was tricky, risky.
If he sent them too soon, she might panic and think
he was creepy. He'd know when the moment was
right. And he needed to extricate himself from this
mess with Tanya, his accuser, first, so Samantha
would know he wasn't some sleazeball. He'd simply
miscalculated. He knew how to treat women; he loved
and respected them. Tanya was the first one he'd ever
read so wrong.

Whatever. Samantha would see his side. Then they
could be together. For now, he'd keep up her sexual
interest with the calls for Johnny. Then segue into the
deeper, more powerful aspects of their inevitable relationship.

When the last fabric wall shut her away from him,
he gave a long sigh, shifted into drive and pulled
away from the curb. After tonight, after interference
by that Jack guy. Rick needed to pick up the pace,
go into higher gear, find out that much sooner everything he could about her likes and dislikes, her passions and tastes and turnoffs. Difficult, yes, but he
relished the challenge. Because he knew in the end
he'd win.

He grinned and beeped his horn in an impulsive
farewell salute as he sped down her block. Johnny
Orion always got the girl.

3

From: Tess Norton
Sent: Friday
To: Samantha Tyler; Erin Thatcher
Subject: re: Readiness

YOU GO GIRL! You aren't going to look pathetic,
you're going to look gorgeous and sexy and oh, so
ripe. BE PICKY! You can have any man you want,
and what you want is someone who can get it up
and keep it up until you're damn ready to call it a
night. Check his feet, his hands, and if they're short
and stubby, move on. If they're long and thick and
his lips are perfect and his…oh, um, sorry. I was
thinking about Dash. Here's the bottom line, kiddo.
This is a present to you. Don't be stingy. Give it all
you've got.
   Love, Tess
   P.S. I want DETAILS

From: Erin Thatcher
Sent: Friday
To: Samantha Tyler; Tess Norton
Subject: re: Readiness

Well, hell! It's about time. And I gotta say it's good
to read a more upbeat you. And, no. You will not

look pathetic. Available is one thing. Available is good. Available will have men flocking. And you'll get to pick and choose your fantasy. If I hadn't already found mine, I think I'd be totally envious! Don't worry about right and perfect and all that relationship crap. Just go find a piece of body candy and spend the night smacking your lips. Oh, and make sure he smacks his!

Love you! Erin

Samantha finished reading the notes, grinned and launched into a new message. Details? She'd give them plenty.

From: Samantha Tyler
Sent: Saturday
To: Erin Thatcher; Tess Norton
Subject: Last Night!

I did it! I went! I met someone! (Is that like I came, I saw, I conquered?) He's totally gorgeous and a Swaggering Butthead to boot. Thinks he's brilliant and is obviously used to the chicks falling at his feet (okay, I was one of them, I couldn't help it). He's a photographer and he wants to photograph me one night next week. Nudge, nudge, wink, wink, say no more!

I feel so good! Like I'm coming out of a coma. I love this. I couldn't fall for this guy in a million years. He's perfect.

I'm so happy!

By the way, have you guys gotten into *When Am-*

ber Burns, yet? Sheesh! No wonder I had sex on the brain. Which guy do you think Amber's going to go for at the end, Adam or Mark—or both at once (ha!)?

Somewhat deliriously,
Samantha

Samantha hit the send button to blast the e-mail off to Erin and Tess, and spun her computer chair to face her home office, arms stretched blissfully wide, an entire Saturday at her disposal. In this mood, staying home doing work wasn't going to cut it. She'd already begun investigating the latest sexual harassment case by interviewing Tanya Banyon, a temp employed by ManForce who brought charges against Rick Grindle. The woman had been convincing, certainly, but Samantha should spend the day preparing for her interview next week with the accused to get his side before she made any decisions.

Samantha rolled her eyes. *Lighten up, woman.* She'd done a million of these cases. Who needed to give up a Saturday afternoon preparing for the expected? She wanted to go out! She wanted to live! She wanted to…shop!

Frankly, her hot-night-out wardrobe was about five years old. She and Brendan had very sensibly dated for two years before they got married, and he'd made it clear she didn't have to dress sexily to be sexy to him. At the time it had seemed so honest, so genuine, so beautiful. Until she recognized it as part of the pattern of suppressing her personality to please him.

God how insidious those little things became when you looked at them as part of the whole.

She *liked* getting dressed up. She liked wearing clothes that flattered her figure. Not like she was trampy. But if she felt good about her clothes and the way she looked, she felt good about herself. If that made her shallow and insecure, tough. She'd made friends with her flaws. At very least, they were loyal company.

Onward! She jumped up and grabbed her purse and keys.

Three hours later, she burst back in through her side door. Success! A black tiny-strapped skintight top with built-in bra, tight stretchy black jeans, and a clingy hot-pink sweater. She hadn't felt this good in ages. Not only clothes, but she'd taken herself out to lunch and the cute guy in the next booth had flirted with her.

She danced into her kitchen, dumped the bags on a chair and grabbed her cell phone to check messages, so full of energy she very nearly got the urge to scrub the floor. This was serious. Maybe she should take some medication.

Her cell phone display showed one missed call; she crossed her fingers, imagining Jack's deep voice, dialed up her voice mail and crossed to get her new clothes out of their bags, so she had something to do if it wasn't him.

"Hello, Johnny Orion. It's Kate. I can't stop thinking about you."

Samantha froze. What was the *deal* with these

women and their faulty dialing habits? And for Pete's
sake, how good could one man *be?*

"I worked all day to cook that dinner for you. But
the look in your eye when you came in…God, I
wasn't hungry for food after that."

Samantha walked to the window, new black camisole clutched in her hand, and stood watching her
garden as if she could somehow see the caller in the
overgrown bushes if she stared hard enough.

"I'll probably never get the sauce out of the rug.
My mom will never forgive me for Aunt Ruby's broken china. And I still have no idea where my thong
is. But ohhhh, Johnny. You were worth it."

Samantha pursed her lips in a silent whistle. An
instant picture came into her head. The door opening.
Johnny Orion standing there—looks by Hugh Jack-
man, body by Russell Crowe, smoldering intensity by
Colin Firth. Male perfection. Slamming the door behind him, head tipped slightly forward as he moved,
so his eyes would shoot passion from under lowered
brows, so he'd have the appearance of a dark, charg-
ing bull.

"I'm still sore, I'm still ragingly horny, I still want
you, Johnny. Call me."

He'd walk forward, and without speaking lift her
in his arms, clear the dining table of its carefully laid
meal with one sweep, clear her body of its carefully
arranged outfit with another, and go to it with hands,
mouth, tongue and—of course—the industrial-sized
penis.

Mmm.

Passion. Sex. Wild passion. Wild sex. She and Brendan never quite got there. There was always something polite in the way they treated each other. Always something slightly apologetic about their lovemaking, as if they felt bad about those pesky animal instincts, and were making do as best they could, since escaping their own humanity was impossible, darn it.

Wild messy passion. Wild messy sex.

She leaned back against the counter, rubbed the shiny camisole top over her body, then downward so it bunched into a soft ball between her legs and she could push against it. Jack might do that for her. The way he'd looked at her in the bar, like he wanted to devour her...

She'd let him.

The top slid between her fingers to the floor; she undid her jeans and pushed her hand inside. Jack Hunter. Right now, in this crazy hormone-charged mood, she wanted him. Badly. She wanted to get naked for him, feel that glorious sense of female power, that explosive chemical reaction at the beginning of an affair, when just the sight of her body would send him into a state of mating-readiness. When the toss of her hips, or the slide of her hands on her own thighs could turn him into a stiff groaning mess of desire. When just the touch of her fingers on his bare skin was enough to get him ready.

She wanted Jack to be her Johnny Orion. To come to her and take his fill of her, giving as much as he took. She wanted that. She wanted it.

Her jeans crept down farther on her straining legs; she rubbed herself harder, breath accelerating, imagining that beautiful meal spread on her dining table, Jack sweeping it to crash on the floor and spreading *her* on the dining table, stripping her, taking her.

"Oh." The orgasm hit, hot and hard and she rode the wave, keeping the image of Jack's naked thrusting body firmly in her mind until she came down, legs cramped and stiff, zipper straining open.

Blanche and Fudge chose that moment to investigate the kitchen and demand dinner in loud no-nonsense yowls.

Samantha blinked and burst out laughing. God what a sight she must be. Masturbating in her own kitchen, fully clothed, in front of her cats. But it didn't feel pathetic. It didn't feel pathetic at all. She pictured Jack again and smiled, doing up her pants, pushing the hair back from her face, body still glowing.

It felt damn good.

"CAN WE GET THE wrinkle out of the left shoulder there?" Jack pointed to the digital image of a Watson Sports T-shirt his assistant Beth handed him. "And try getting the folds to run left to right instead. Maybe straighten that seam a little more. I like the look, but the client won't want the logo distorted. That should do it. Let me know when it's set and I'll shoot it."

"Done." Beth pointed to another table where a prop stylist was lovingly adjusting Watson golf shoes on a small mat of Astroturf. "They're ready for you to check the shoes."

Jack wandered over, hands in his pockets, whistling carelessly through his teeth, eyed the shoes critically and nodded. ''Looking good—I like the angle. Let me see a test when it's ready.''

He strolled back past the T-shirt table, still whistling, a rambling melody completely at odds with the techno-pop assaulting the studio's airspace, and stopped to check the next shot—a putter to be shot on outline, against a neutral color for the client to fit into its own background.

Unfortunately, with no one else at the table demanding he do his job, no matter how hard he focused his eyes, his brain refused to take in the concept of ''golf club.'' Thoughts of *her* invaded immediately, as they'd been invading all weekend no matter how hard he tried either to push them away or sort out the dilemma to a workable solution.

He should call her today. He probably should have called her over the weekend. Samantha was perfect for the human dining table series. Tall, slender, not overly curved. More than that, she had the perfect look. Class, innocence, sensuality, all built into the striking planes of her face, so that even immobile and deadpan, those qualities would come through in the shot.

So why hesitate? He absently adjusted the head of the putter, which a barely conscious part of him knew didn't need adjusting.

Because he wanted her. Because in her classy innocent sensuality, she represented a danger to the control he held tight to. Since Krista he'd been careful to find models who fit the shots but held little or no appeal for him personally. He wasn't going down that road again.

But something about this woman called strongly to him. Made him plenty aware that being alone with her in a studio—even on a closed set with a hair and makeup stylist on call—while Samantha had on next to nothing would bring temptation home.

More than temptation. Torture.

He should avoid her. Listen to the voice in his head shouting, "Run, you idiot, run." He didn't need to mess up his life again, now that he'd clawed his way back on track. If he slept with her, as he was pretty sure she wanted him to by the signals she was sending out, and if he got away with it this time, then what would stop him the next time someone offered, and the next? Until he hooked up with another Krista and had his career nuked again. He might not be able to start over a third time and get anywhere he or anyone else could respect.

Jack glared at the putter and unnecessarily adjusted the grip this time. What scared him was that in spite of the well-known, acknowledged, been-down-that-road-before risks, he wanted Samantha in his studio and in his series. He missed the game, the chase, the thrilling, orgasmic victory. He *wanted* to be tempted by her. Wanted to feel the intense rush of excitement as he had in the bar. A rush he'd denied himself for so long.

He felt like a recovering alcoholic face-to-foam with a big frosty mug of beer. Lifting it, inhaling the sour yeasty scent, bringing it to his lips so the bubbles tickled his—

"What the heck is with you?" His studio manager Maria lifted a dark pierced eyebrow. "You've been whackyed-out all day."

"Whackyed-out?" He smiled at her tough hands-on-hips stance, so incongruous on her tiny frame. But he sure as hell wouldn't want to be on the receiving end of her temper. "How have I been whackyed-out?"

"All day you've been wandering and whistling. Usually you're like a headless chicken running around."

"Wow, Maria, thanks." He sent her a look of fond exasperation. "It really pumps me up to be compared to barnyard animals."

"No problem." She crossed her arms over her chest and tapped her foot. "So what's this woman's name?"

Jack tried very hard to recover from extreme shock without giving himself away. "What woman?"

Maria's eyes narrowed. "The one who has you whackyed-out."

"I don't know what you're—"

"Ha! Cut the crap." She leaned forward and impaled him with her nearly black eyes. "You can fool some people sometimes, but Maria never. I know you have a woman and she's crazying up your head. My brother Paulo looks just like that about ten times a year. If my Miguel looks like that even for half an hour, bam!" She made a decisive chop on her open palm.

He grinned and shook his head. "And if I tell you it's none of your business?"

"I'm making it my business." She cocked her head so the studio light sparkled off the diamond piercing her nostril. "She better be worth you. Is she?"

He pictured Samantha's blond hair draping her shoulders, her soft-looking, slightly rosy skin, clear eyes dancing with life. She was probably worth about ten of him. "I don't know."

"Then you better find out." She made a circling motion with one finger next to her multi-earringed ear. "Or you'll stay wacky forever."

He crossed his arms over his chest. "Is that right."

"I'm *serious*." Her eyes widened in outrage. "This obsession won't go away by itself. Like a splinter, she will dig in deeper if you ignore her. Take her out. Examine. You can't get free any other way."

He rolled his eyes, still grinning. Since the dawn of time, there had never been a more determined matchmaker. "I think you're reading a little too much into it."

She shrugged. "If you don't give love a chance at the obvious time, it'll come back and bite you in the ass."

"Love?" He stared at her incredulously. Over the top, even for Maria. "This isn't love we're talking about."

"Oh, right, matters of the dick." She waved at him dismissively. "I've seen you lusting plenty of times.

This is different. You watch. You'll see. In one year, I'll be dancing at your wedding, thumbing my nose at you.''

Jack laughed. As much as he sometimes wanted to use dynamite to budge her from her strongly adhered-to opinions, Maria lit up the studio like a 2K hot light, and he adored her. ''My wedding, huh?''

''You betcha. You blow this you'll end up alone in a cold apartment with a shriveled you-know-what, eating cold ravioli out of a can.''

''Well, if you put it *that* way, I better give it some serious thought.'' Jack rubbed his thumb along the side of his jaw, pretending to be giving it some serious thought. All kidding aside, and he owed Maria thanks for bringing him face-to-face with the truth this morning, he'd spent the last few days fooling himself thinking he was trying to decide. He'd made his decision about ten seconds after he saw Samantha sitting in the bar, rigid with nerves over being out by herself. She was too perfect for the shoot not to call.

At the same time, he was smart to recognize the rush of fight or flight energy, like a swimmer seeing shadows in the water under him, not knowing if they were coral reefs or hungry sharks. No question he had a struggle ahead to keep the relationship professional.

''Well.'' He sighed, long and loud. ''If you've made up your mind, Maria, then it's obvious what I have to do.''

Maria nodded firmly, her lips starting a smile that reflected his mischief. ''Damn right.''

''I guess…'' He shrugged in exaggerated helplessness and let his hands slap down on his thighs. "I guess I have no choice but to call her."

"Ms. Tyler? Sorry to keep you waiting. I'm Rick Grindle."

Samantha looked up from the file she'd been studying in the reception area of Eisemann, Inc.

Yikes.

Her nice-to-meet-you smile immediately threatened to slide off her lips and she had to use extra muscle to bolster it back up. Whatever she'd expected Rick Grindle to look like, this wasn't it. The man was well over six feet and built like a linebacker. The way Tanya, his accuser, had talked about him, Samantha had expected something closer to Elmer Fudd.

His eyes were an intense pale gray set off by the pure white of his shirt and the deeper-gray charcoal of his perfectly tailored suit. The black-and-white impression was marred by a crimson tie that made a silk blood-swath down into his neatly buttoned jacket. His hair had started to go the way of bald things and he kept what was left buzzed military-short. Unlike some guys, the lack of hair reinforced his virility and completed the picture of the imposing giant.

"Hello, Mr. Grindle. Thanks for seeing me today."

She stood to shake his hand, searching his face for whatever character traits might be visible. His face showed no emotion, nothing but a quiet polite contemplation of her, as if he had interesting, perceptive and intelligent thoughts buzzing in his balding skull, at odds with the impression his brutish build gave.

Ten seconds later, Samantha of the Iron Gaze had stooped to pick up her briefcase as an excuse to look away. He was probably the most overwhelmingly masculine man she'd ever met. Possibly a predator. Possibly attractive to someone like Tanya. Up to Samantha to get at the truth.

"Right this way." He gestured toward the door to his office, carpeted forest-green with floor-to-ceiling bookcases providing color and richness behind a massive oak desk. "And please call me Rick."

Samantha passed his huge body on her way in, startled to feel herself react physically. Not sexually, nothing like she'd felt around Jack, who still hadn't called, damn him, but an awareness, a strange unsettling ripple in her mood and consciousness, so quick she couldn't identify whether the sensation had been pleasant or not.

"Please, have a seat."

"Thank you." She took one of the green leather and polished wood chairs arranged precisely in front of the desk, which had a nearly empty in-box, a stapler, a blotting pad and a paper clip holder, all standing at perfect right angles. A pot of ivy sat on one corner, leaves trailing attractively onto the wooden desktop. Next to it, one perfect red rose in a slender white porcelain bud vase.

She felt the giant move around behind her until his elegantly dressed body came into view and her visual perception took over. He sat smoothly at his desk, folded his powerful hands on the green-bordered deskpad and waited.

Samantha opened her file into the silence, shocked to notice her hands trembling. During interviews she counted on being in charge, to make sure the interviewee knew there was no getting around her. In front of this man, she felt like a schoolgirl in the principal's office.

"How can I help you?" His voice held no hint of impatience or dread, rather a cordial warmth that made it sound as if he'd rearranged his entire day just so he could have the pleasure of her company.

Deal, Samantha. She clamped down hard on her mood and emotions to become the controlled, objective, observant person she needed to be to weigh his version of the story against the one she'd already heard. "You are familiar with the accusations of Tanya Banyon?"

Rick's full lips tightened briefly, not in anger so much as regret and embarrassment. "Yes, I am."

"I need to go over certain details of your encounters with her to get your statement on what you remember, how you intended your words and actions, versus how Ms. Banyon perceived them."

He nodded. "Very good."

Samantha let him sit under her outwardly nonchalant scrutiny for a count of five. His gray gaze held hers, calm, attentive, waiting for her questions. No squirming. No fidgeting fingers. One point for him. During her brief initial interview with Samantha, Tanya had been a nervous wreck.

"On the morning of July tenth, Ms. Banyon alleges that you touched her in an inappropriate manner as she bent over to drink at the water fountain. She says that when she confronted you, you did not deny that you touched her.''

''No. I didn't deny it.'' He leaned back in his chair and put his still-folded hands into his lap. ''I was putting a memo in a file and it slipped out of my hands. I made a grab for it and missed. I was very embarrassed and apologized immediately. She obviously didn't believe it was an accident.''

''I see.'' Samantha put irony into her voice as if she didn't believe him either and waited. No further clarification, not a trace of defensiveness crept into his eyes. Silences generally proved fatal to the guilty. ''Ms. Banyon also alleges that you said, 'You can teach me to grab your ass anytime.' Is that true?''

He drew a deep breath as if the memory pained him and tented his fingers under his lips. ''She was hostile. She whirled around after my apology and said, 'I'll teach you to grab my ass.' I was taken aback as you can imagine and, I admit, angry. No one wants to be accused over an honest mistake. What I said to her, by way of dismissal, was, 'Perhaps you can teach me to grab your ass another time, Ms. Banyon.'''

He enunciated the words ''grab your ass'' as if they belonged to a foreign language. Samantha could just imagine the expression on his face when he had to say it by the water fountain. As if he was being forced to step in dog poop in nine-hundred-dollar shoes. Maybe Tanya had misinterpreted, or tried to cover her own sins. But of course there was always…maybe not. Interesting case.

"Ms. Banyon also alleges that during the month of July, on several occasions, you looked at her inappropriately, that you repeatedly asked her out in spite of her persistent refusals, and that on one occasion you used sexually suggestive language."

Samantha looked up from her file to the most genuinely baffled expression she'd seen in a long time. If this guy was lying, he was a champ.

"I—there may have been times I asked her to join a group of us for lunch..." He furrowed his thick, well-groomed brows. "Once we had been working late, we were both exhausted and I suggested we get something to eat so we could recharge our batteries...but asking her out as in man-woman on a date? No."

Samantha made a note on her file. "The sexually suggestive language?"

He sighed, spun his office chair around and searched the bookcase behind him. "I have a feeling I know what that's about. Do you know the work of Colin Bedgers? An English essayist of the mid-twentieth century who wrote a few short stories and some poetry. Here it is."

He pulled down a thin black volume stamped with gold lettering and flipped through the pages. "Ms. Banyon had replied to my request for filing information with the phrase, 'you can stick it where the sun don't shine.' Which reminded me of a passage in this story and I quoted it to her." He flipped pages back and forth a few more times, then handed the book to Samantha, leaning forward to indicate the place as she accepted the book.

She looked down at the text, marked by a huge masculine finger with clean-trimmed nails, and felt that strange stirring of awareness again. What the hell was that?

I could, if I wanted, even in your darkness find sun and light and relief from the burden of being.

She looked up expectantly from the passage.

Rick shrugged. "The story is about finding the good in all of us. I thought to recast her rude comment into something more pleasant. Obviously she missed my intent."

Samantha handed the book back to him. "And the 'inappropriate looking'?"

He twisted his mouth in a smile that bloomed into a grin. Incredibly, a blush started up his cheeks. Samantha waited politely, on alert at the unexpected sight. So the guy wasn't made of steel after all.

"Ms. Banyon," he cleared his throat, "has, on occasion, worn clothing that, shall we say, emphasizes her…"

A snort of laughter nearly escaped Samantha's forced composure. *Assets?*

Rick pulled at his tie, the blush deepening. "One day she wore a bright yellow low-cut top with a push-up bra. Believe me, the entire *office* was looking. Even the women. You just couldn't get around it."

"I see." Samantha understood. For her initial interview with Samantha, Tanya had dressed like a stripper on break. Most people in her situation knocked themselves out to appear conventional. Samantha couldn't count the number of convent-girl outfits and conservative suits she'd seen in sexual harassment interviews that obviously didn't belong to the uncomfortable wearer.

"For some reason she picked me out and made some unpleasant remark." He unbuttoned his jacket, leaned back and put his hands to his hips, exposing an unwrinkled shirtfront over a trim waist. "Ms. Tyler, I have come to wonder through all this...that is, I wondered for a time whether Ms. Banyon was...attracted to me."

"Really." Samantha blinked away from taking in his impressive physique, her instincts jumping. Classic defense move of guilty harassers was to charge the harrassee with being a scorned admirer. Except the look on Rick's face was anything but guilty or conniving. He was clearly mortified, as if he expected Samantha to laugh at the mere idea of anyone finding him attractive.

"Maybe I sound egotistical. But a man of my age knows when a woman is putting out signals. And I believe she was."

"How did you react to these...signals."

"I was polite, but clearly uninterested." Rick folded his big hands back on his desk, regarding her calmly, his blush fading.

"Did Ms. Banyon say or do anything concrete to lead you to think she was coming onto you?"

"No." He shook his head, mouth bunched regretfully. "I'm sorry. It wasn't that overt. Just...signals."

"Which you didn't respond to."

"No."

"How long was she sending these signals? And can you be more specific about what they were and how you responded?"

"Let's see." He frowned in concentration. "A couple of weeks, maybe more. Things like maintaining eye contact longer than necessary, tilting her head to one side to expose her neck, playing with her hair, standing closer than a professional situation warranted, letting…body parts brush against me."

She monitored him carefully. Still nothing that would indicate to her experienced eye that he was lying or uncomfortable with his words. "And your response?"

"I pretended it wasn't happening. If she kept the eye contact going, I'd smile and thank her for her good work on whatever job she had done. If she was too close, I'd move away. I never encouraged her. In fact, the more I avoided her, the more obvious the signals became. It was getting to the point where I felt I'd have to say something when she abruptly stopped and started getting hostile instead."

"Do you recall what happened right before she stopped and allegedly got hostile?"

"No, I'm afraid I don't. I don't think there was any one event." He took a long breath, searching the ceiling with a troubled expression. "Ms. Banyon is a recent divorcée. Within the last year."

Something, maybe the touch of pity in his quiet, even voice made Samantha's body stiffen into raised-fur mode, ready to hiss, and if necessary, scratch his eyes out. "I'm sorry, I don't follow."

"I've watched several friends and my sister go through it. There is a period following the break-up..." He shifted forward in his seat and looked down to meet her eyes.

Samantha forced herself to stare back into those pale gray circles. Her body reacted again. Not exactly pleasure, not exactly distaste, but a reaction. Something stopped her short of real attraction.

"Sometimes right after the break-up, sometimes a few months later, there is a period of heightened... sexuality."

Samantha swallowed convulsively and hated herself for it. He noticed, she was sure. His eyes flicked down to her throat and then back to her eyes.

"I see. So you think Tanya was going through that...period?"

"It's possible. My sister is usually a very modest and conservative person. After her divorce, for a few months, she started dressing provocatively, going out to bars to find dates, nothing like her usual behavior."

Samantha's underarms started to get damp and prickly. It was all she could do to sit still and listen. God, how humiliating. Her big busting-out freeing-herself moment that felt so vibrant and alive—and she was just a statistic someone else felt sorry for. Had Jack picked up on the post-divorce bust-out phenomenon? Did he go home, call all his friends and say, whoa, baby, she signals like a diesel engine, I am home free. Guffaw, guffaw. Virtual high fives all around.

"I see." She gritted her teeth and told herself to stop saying *I see.*

"I've seen the same in my friends. It passes, then they revert to type." He didn't take his eyes off her. He must be able to see her discomfort. What the hell was he doing? What the hell was he thinking? What the hell had happened to this interview?

"You make it sound like a temporary mental illness." She tried to keep her voice amused, not accusing, and wasn't sure she succeeded. "You don't think it's a real part of their personality reasserting itself?"

He turned his head just slightly at her question, chin tilted, as if he was taking in the significance of her remark.

She clamped off the rest of her thought. *Don't go there, Samantha, you're giving yourself away.*

"Mental illness? Of course not." He spoke as if he didn't find her comments odd. Maybe he was too polite to let on. "It's entirely understandable. Suddenly after years in a miserable marriage, feeling trapped, suffocated, you're free to take on the world that you believed was denied to you till death did you part. I'm sure it's intoxicating, empowering, freeing… fabulous."

She forced herself to look down at the file now bent and worried along its edges from her death-grip. *Oh my God.* His voice was low, impersonal, but strangely seductive, as if his words were meant for her situation instead of Tanya's. As if he understood everything she'd been living and feeling for the past two years. She'd never heard a male talk so openly about emotional matters that didn't concern his own needs. Were there really men capable of that depth of empathy? Brendan had the emotional perceptiveness of a crustacean. Jack of the Missing Dialing Finger was doubtless the same.

"I see." She winced. "I understand."

"This is the time to explore, to try out people or things that appeal simply on the basis of the fact that they do appeal, without thought of ever-after, or even tomorrow."

She lifted her hand to cut him off before he made her into a complete basket case. In all her years of interviewing, she'd never, ever allowed any emotion deeper than sympathy or mild disgust to intrude. Now she wasn't even sure what she was feeling, only that it was rattling and profound and she had to get an immediate grip or risk spilling her life's troubles to his apparently sympathetic and understanding ear. "So you think Ms. Banyon was going through this sexual…liberation, and came onto you?"

"It's possible. I certainly don't hold it against her. But casual affairs don't interest me." His eyebrows rose toward each other, his forehead creased, making this giant hulk of a man look boyish and vulnerable. "If a woman comes to me, I want her with a smile on her lips that only I can put there, and the possibility of forever carried in her heart."

He said the words calmly, without a trace of irony

or self-consciousness. Samantha pursed her lips to keep her jaw from dropping, while a shockingly fierce longing put her insides in a vice. She had never heard a man say anything that romantic in her life and apparently mean it. Brendan had been a cum laude graduate of the "That Was Great, Baby" school of romance. Jack, Swaggering Butthead Extraordinaire, would probably be even worse—though to be fair, she was interested in him for just that reason.

Maybe Tanya, in her post-divorce instability, had gotten sick of the Jacks of the world not calling. Maybe she'd sensed the romantic quality in this man which Samantha had just glimpsed, maybe his quiet soft-spoken confidence and intelligence had been the antithesis of Tanya's ex and she'd focused her bust-out boldness on this man. When he'd rejected her, understanding where her attraction originated, maybe Tanya had turned her embarrassment into anger and thirst for revenge. It wouldn't be the first time, doubtless wouldn't be the last. At this point anything was possible. She'd need to further the investigation before she'd be convinced either way.

"Thank you, Rick."

He shot her one of those charming smiles and she had to concentrate on tucking papers back into her file and the file back into her briefcase. The guy unnerved her, no question. And she didn't unnerve easily. "That's all I have today. I appreciate your time in this matter."

"No trouble at all, Ms. Tyler." He walked her to the door, opened it and offered his hand which she took, feeling as if her fingers disappeared entirely into the warm firm grip of his. "I'm sure this... misunderstanding can be cleared up quickly."

"I hope so." Samantha left his office, admittedly relieved to be out of his magnetic and draining presence, and walked out into the polished-wood and cream-colored linoleum hallway that smelled like cleaning fluid. She wasn't going to say so, but considering how she'd walked into this interview all but convinced Tanya was telling the truth, and walked out all but convinced Rick was, if he wanted it cleared up quickly, he'd better order a miracle.

In the elevator on the way down from the fourteenth floor of the Sears Tower, she dragged her cell phone out of her bag and checked the display. Missed call—one. The number was unfamiliar.

Her heart started pounding and she told herself severely to calm the hell down at the same time she practically spilled the entire contents of her purse digging through it for his business card. She held it next to the display to compare numbers, and her pounding heart started doing a graceful up-tempo swing number.

Jack.

4

From: Tess Norton
Sent: Monday
To: Samantha Tyler; Erin Thatcher
Subject: re: Last Night!

Oh, Samantha! You diva! Way to take charge of your own life, girl. A photographer? Hmm, could be very exciting. And don't forget you can send pictures to us, please! Well, not those pictures. Sheesh. Get your mind out of the bedroom.

On second thought, leave it there.

Gentle reminder: he's not *the one* and therefore, he is the perfect man for you to experiment with. Haul all your secret fantasies out and go for it. What have you got to lose?

I'm just thrilled for you, honey!

Oh, and about *When Amber Burns*, I started it. Was interrupted by Dash who insisted we play Hide the Salami, and I haven't gotten back to the book yet. Not that I'm complaining, mind you. :)

Love, Tess

From: Erin Thatcher
Sent: Monday

To: Samantha Tyler; Tess Norton
Subject: re: Last Night!

Well, delirious sounds as good as delicious, girl-friend! Whoo-hoo! And falling at his feet is perfect. It puts you right in line to enjoy his, uh, assets!! But a photographer? Is that as clichéd as coming up to see his etchings????? At least you're not in a gullible frame of mind, mistaking that line for anything but exactly what it is. (Suggestion: Wear a kinky mask so that if you end up on the Internet, no one will recognize your face!)

To tell you the truth, I haven't even started the book yet, grrr! I've had so much going on at school. But I'm loving it so I really can't complain. Sebastian starts a new book tour this next week and will be gone for at least ten days—sob! sob!—so I'll definitely read it then...though if it's as hot as you say I might not want to read it while he's out of town! What's a sex-crazed girl to do!!!!

Love you! Erin

Samantha bit her lip and closed Erin's e-mail. A mask? In case she ended up on the Internet? Okay, that was about the last thing she wanted to hear. She glanced at her watch again, even though she promised herself thirty seconds before that she'd stop all the watch-glancing. A whole half hour before she had to leave for Jack's studio.

After finding his message on her cell phone Monday after the interview with Rick, she'd made herself wait several hours so Jack wouldn't think—okay, wouldn't *know*—how eager she was. Unfortunately, the passing time had upped her tension and excitement to the point where she'd had to do deep breathing exercises before she could dial his number.

His voice had been deeper than she remembered, but its effect was the same. Electric shivers down to her toes. A wild high to her mood. Fantasies about what they could accomplish together in the sack. At the same time, actually talking to him, trying her best to keep her conversation smooth and casual, had taken him out of the realm of Exciting Possibility and made her realize with total clarity that he was a complete stranger and that she was planning to sleep with him.

In a word, *eek*.

She pressed "send/receive" on her Outlook Express, hoping for another nice distracting e-mail to kill more time, maybe some thoughtful comments about this month's book choice for the Eve's Apple reading club. Nothing. These thirty minutes were going to kill her. She couldn't remember ever being this tense over her early dates with Brendan. Excited, hell yes. But Brendan had been so calm and comforting and easy to talk to—so easy she didn't notice they never talked about anything intimate or important—that she hadn't really worked herself up over going to meet him. At least not to this degree.

Granted, tonight was also a foray into uncharted territory. A date with a man she was interested in only physically, and to hell with how easy he was to talk to. Where the activity planned for the date was unspoken, but understood. In a way the assumption made everything simpler by taking away the "would it or wouldn't it, will she or won't she" agony, but it also made everything more nervous. If a normal, get-to-know-him date went badly, she could end the evening early. If sex was going badly, it was a little more difficult to extract herself. *Gee, you know, your relentless thrusting is swell, but I have to get home and brush my cats.*

Still, she hadn't made a commitment to sex except in her own mind. Nothing had been set in concrete. The point of the evening was still purportedly photography. So if anything didn't feel right before they got going, she could walk away.

But God, she hoped it would feel right. She hadn't been touched in so long. Even a few kisses, or the possessive warm feel of a man's hands on her back would make the evening worth it. Though frankly, once she experienced warm possessive hands, she was bound to get greedy for the rest of the show. Sex was something she loved, that she was good at. Having a successful—sexessful?—evening would do wonders to boost her self-esteem. Maybe this post-divorce wanton period was pathetic to a romantic like Rick Grindle. But it sure as hell felt good and right and important to her.

Samantha glanced at her watch again and winced. Only three minutes worth of pondering. That wasn't going to take up nearly enough of her nervous-waiting time. She got up from her computer chair and wandered through the dining room, grimacing at the pile of bills, magazines and unanswered mail on the table. *Go bug someone else's conscience.*

In the living room she found *When Amber Burns* and settled in to read. The heroine, Amber, was torn between Mark, the sweet earnest guy who wanted to marry her, and Adam, the hot sexy number who promised her passion, but for how long? Samantha had left Amber and Mark on the way to a nice day on a private island beach, but she had a feeling Adam would show up somehow. What author would want to waste a private island beach when tall, dark and hung-like-a-horse could be available for action with a flick of her typing fingers?

One chapter and roughly twenty minutes later, Samantha put the book down. *Oh. My. God.* Mark had a very convenient allergy attack and Amber very conveniently stayed on the beach, in the nude of course, and Adam very conveniently—oh, but who cared about too much convenience.

The sex-athon was so beautifully written, so overwhelmingly passionate and in-your-face erotic, that Samantha even forgot her usual what-about-the-sand-in-her-butt objections to those kinds of scenes.

Very, very hot.

She put her hands to her flushed cheeks and grinned. To put it mildly, she was suddenly extremely eager to get over to Jack's studio and check out his shutter speed. If Amber could do it, so could Samantha. She should be celebrating her reemergence into sexual circulation, not cowering at home with nerves. The girls were right. She deserved this evening.

Her Men To Do hour had arrived.

JACK ADJUSTED THE LIGHTS, which he'd already adjusted, and checked his rolls of film, which he'd already checked. Maybe he could spend some *more* time doing unnecessary things so he wouldn't have to face how on edge he was. Like quadruple-check the props for the pose which George had prepared earlier, during the regular workday.

Samantha would arrive shortly. He'd scheduled a half hour for them to talk, for her to get comfortable, drink a glass of wine and relax, until Jenny arrived to do her hair and makeup and they could get started.

By the time he called her on Monday he'd convinced himself that, Maria's opinion on Samantha's role as a splinter notwithstanding, he'd blown his attraction out of proportion. It made sense. The offer of a ménage à trois with Yvette and Vanessa that evening last week had started his thoughts in certain directions, and the sight of Samantha had merely escalated them. Jack was a professional. This series was important to him. He wasn't going to let his dick run or ruin his career, especially not a second time.

The gentle chime of the doorbell shot adrenaline through him. Samantha. He buzzed her into the building, strode past the reception area and waited until the elevator doors opened and she stepped out.

Damn.

A smile he couldn't help sprang onto his face; his

stomach took an open-ended swan dive. She was gorgeous. Absolutely gorgeous. Confident and poised in a dynamite tight black camisole under a magenta cardigan that contrasted stunningly with the blue of her eyes. She was perfect. For the shot.

"Come in." He stepped back and gestured her into the studio, letting his eyes drop—only once to satisfy his curiosity—to her shapely rear, filling out form-fitting black pants that looked soft and comfortable and chic at the same time. He followed her into the reception area and stood, hands on his hips, watching her take in her surroundings.

She was nervous. Her confident body language was still going full force, but he noticed now the fist clutching her purse, a slightly anxious tilt of her brows, a brief hesitation of where to pose her feet, a tentative hand pushing blond hair back behind her ear.

A strange warming of his insides startled him and he pushed it away. If she was nervous, so much the better. This woman wasn't Krista the Bulldozer. Easier this way to stay in control and make the evening go exactly as it should.

"What do you think?" He knew he sounded proud. He was proud. The studio was impressive.

She turned to face him and he reacted again to the energetic light in her complicated blue eyes. "It's bigger than I thought it would be."

"You know, women say that to me all the time." He grinned, expecting rolling-eyed laughter.

Instead, she quirked one eyebrow and gave a smile

that made Mona Lisa look brassy and obvious. "How nice to hear."

Jack opened his mouth to respond, and when absolutely no appropriate response would exit his mouth, he closed it.

She smiled again, a smile so sweet he could see the devil in it, and moved farther into the room. "So, Jack. Where do you...want me?"

Jack froze for a heartbeat, then forced himself to move toward the reception area couch. *Where do you want me?* Did she think something more than photography tonight was a sure thing? That was all he needed.

"I thought we could relax a little first, chat for a bit, maybe have a glass of wine. Jenny will be here in about half an hour and then we can get started."

She turned toward him and managed to sweep an incredulous look off her face a split second after he saw it. "Jenny?"

"Makeup." He pointed to her face, then higher. "Hair."

"Oh, of course."

He could swear she looked disappointed. Had she just wanted to come here for sex? Had he put out that much of a vibe at the bar? He'd flirted with her, sure, just as she had with him, but his overall intentions were professional.

Old habits died hard. He must have gone into enough of his old routine that she misunderstood. And hell, he did want her. No question about that. But wanting and doing something about it were two different things in his life, now. Maybe he should have made that clearer.

When he sent her home after the shoot, she'd probably think he was a no-balled jerk, inviting her up for a "session" and then delivering only artistic intentions. So be it. He'd been called worse.

"Have a seat." He gestured to the sofa in the reception area and went back into the kitchen off the back of the studio for the wine he'd taken more pains than usual to select. Old Mr. Heiden at The Wine Enthusiast had raised an eyebrow at Jack's uncharacteristic indecision, then winked when he handed him the bottle with some "special night" comment that made Jack feel like a teenager buying condoms at the corner drugstore.

And speaking of condoms, he'd made very sure there wasn't so much as a wrapper of one in the studio.

He uncorked the 1998 Côtes du Rhône and poured an experimental half inch into her glass. No booze for him. Nothing that could cloud his concentration or, God forbid, soften his resolve. He swirled the crimson liquid and inhaled the bouquet. Nice. Medium-bodied, not sweet, not acid. Like her.

He poured the glass full and brought it out to her.

"You're not having any?"

"Not while I'm working." He considered sitting next to her on the sofa and chose the overstuffed armchair instead. "I need my brain fully functional to get the shots right."

"Understood." She gave him that killer half smile again. "Maybe…later?"

He held her gaze, taking in the signals buzzing around his body, knowing he should say *not tonight,* but wanting to get sucked into the game. She was so damn sexy. "We'll see how I feel."

"Okay." She lifted the glass in a toast, head tilted to one side so her hair hung heavy and free, exposing her neck and the beginning slope of one shoulder, perfect fair skin contrasting with the vibrant color of her sweater. "Here's to seeing how you feel."

Her voice was low and suggestive. Jack clenched his teeth together. *Chat, Jack. Just. Chat.*

"So, how are things in the sexual harassment arena?"

"Complicated." She smiled and took a sip of the wine. "Mmm, that's nice."

"Glad you like it." He hated it when sexy women said, "mmm." It made him imagine all kinds of other ways he could get her to say the same thing. "Complicated how?"

She pressed her lips together, drew her hand up and down along the dark blue armrest of the sofa.

He wasn't even going to *begin* thinking about how he hated watching sexy women stroke furniture.

"I'm working on an unusual case right now." She shook her hair back from her face and took another sip. "I can usually tell who's lying and who's telling the truth, or at least where the misunderstanding occurred. This one's very peculiar."

"They both seem like liars or they both seem honest?"

"Honest." She drew her brows down and gave her head a little confused shake. "It's disorienting. I'm generally a good judge of character."

"And in this case?"

"The man…he—well, she portrayed him as lecherous, and he came across to me, initially anyway, as intelligent, sincere, sort of a…hopeless romantic."

She shrugged, raised her hand and let it flop back down onto the armrest before she started her stroking motion again. A blush made its way up her cheek. Something about this guy intrigued her? Attracted her? An irrational stab of jealousy shocked him. What was that about? He wasn't going to get involved with her. She could feel whatever she wanted about other men.

"Maybe he's harassing her in a hopelessly romantic way."

Samantha laughed, that warm rich laugh that made something strangely nonsexual happen inside him. "Now there's a possibility."

"You like hopeless romantics?" He leaned forward and rested his arms on his thighs, watching her sip her drink and consider her answer. He loved watching her. Her face was incredibly expressive. He had the feeling she couldn't hide a single emotion if she tried. The camera would eat her up.

"I haven't met many. Not men anyway. No offense."

"None taken. Are you a hopeless romantic?"

"Me?" She thumped a hand to her chest, nearly choking on her wine. "Hardly. I doubt you'll find many divorced hopeless romantics. Most of us are pretty cynical."

"I don't know." He narrowed his eyes and studied her. "If you were truly cynical you'd still be married. But you left to find something better."

"What makes you think that?"

"You mean you're not looking for Mr. Right, Part Two?" He wasn't even sure why he wanted to know.

"Not now anyway." She took a sip of wine, keeping her clear eyes on him over the rim of her glass. "Right now, I'm looking for fun."

Bam. Walked right into that one. Adrenaline and arousal fought to take control, urging him to jump in with both feet. *You want fun? I can show you fun.* He could tell by the ease with which Samantha inhabited her body, that she would probably take "fun" to an incredible level.

"Fun is good." He kept his voice light and searched for a way to derail the subject before it got out of hand. "So you don't think men can be hopeless romantics."

"They can act in romantic ways, but I haven't met any who were that way to the core. Except maybe that one guy, and he could well be full of it. Why?" She lifted an eyebrow and tilted her head again in that take-me way she had that drove him nuts. "Are *you* a hopeless romantic?"

"Me?" He thumped his hand to his chest in mischievous imitation of her earlier gesture. "Hardly."

"The love 'em and leave 'em type?"

"That's more like it." He grinned. "Disgusting, huh."

She shrugged. "Men like you have their uses."

"Oh we do." He folded his arms across his chest, taking up her laughing-eyed challenge in spite of the warning signals flashing through his brain. "And do I dare ask what those uses would be?"

"You better not."

A flicker of uncertainty ran through her eyes and he had to suppress that strange twisting sensation. As long as she was the confident seductress, bluffing or not, he could play the flirtatious sparring game untouched. But her nerves or fear brought out a strange need to put her at ease, find out why she had really come here tonight, what she was out to prove, either to him or to herself.

"No? Why is that?"

"Because…" She was in control again, arching her brows, leaning back against the couch as if she was offering him her body, keeping her wineglass close to her lips. "The answer might surprise you."

He couldn't let that pass. "I doubt that very much."

"Oh?" Her nostrils jumped, her eyes grew luminous; she swallowed. Jack's lungs tightened. He'd invited this. He'd come to this evening telling himself he'd be thoroughly professional and he'd nearly blown it in less than half an hour. The woman was lethal.

"What if I said that guys like you can satisfy the needs of a woman like me."

Easy, Jack. "A woman like you?"

She took a slow sip of wine and pulled the glass away, the liquid painting her lips to shining ruby. "Divorced. Alone. And needy. Very needy, Jack."

His body reacted predictably. Shit. He was going in deep.

"Samantha—"

"At my house…in my bedroom…above my bed, guess what I have?"

He eased his hips slowly up, then down, trying to find a more comfortable position. "A mirror."

"No." She ran her tongue around the rim of her glass. It looked long and warm and wet. His eyes got hard and hot. So did his cock.

"Guess again."

"I give up."

She leaned forward so her breasts swelled up, round and soft and inviting against the taut material of her camisole under the gold necklace she'd worn in the bar. "Jack…"

He gripped the armrest of his chair. "Yes."

"My ceiling fan doesn't work. You know how to fix those?"

He didn't move. His brain was having to shift gears very fast and his body wasn't sure it could follow. *"What?"*

She smiled, a quick smile that curved her lips up and dropped them back down. Then she winked. And smiled again. "I told you I had needs."

He dropped his head onto his hands and groaned. Man, had she gotten him. "Do you have any idea what you just did to me?"

She burst out laughing, not the sexy rich chuckle that undid him, but clean honest laughter of enjoyment that undid him more. "I'm sorry. I couldn't resist. I'm actually kidding about needing help with the fan—I plan to learn how to fix it myself."

He grinned to show he could take a joke, though he was tempted to bend her over the couch as punishment. "An independent woman."

"That's me." She lifted her wine in a toast and drained it.

"More?"

She shook her head quickly, then gave her glass a wistful glance.

"You sure?"

"Mmm…maybe a little."

He took her glass back to the kitchen, still rattled by his reaction to her teasing. This was a woman who knew what she wanted, and by the looks of it, how to go about getting it. Plenty of women like her in that regard. He was in little danger from them. But what could make Samantha serious trouble were the signs of nerves and uncertainty under her confidence, the seduction that turned into a big ha-ha joke before it got out of hand. As if she was out of practice and needed to get her bearings before she pulled out the big guns.

His reaction to that vulnerability made her dangerous, where other women were merely pleasant temptations. And she hadn't even taken her clothes off yet for the shoot.

He recorked the wine and leaned both hands on the counter to take a moment of regroup time. *Breathe in. Breathe out.*

He was in control. Jennifer would be here soon and he would be able to disappear into his art the second he got started, as he always did. Samantha would change from a danger to his sanity and career into a dining table, and his obsession would become only capturing her image on film.

A few shots, his furniture series taken one step further, and he'd call it a night.

5

JENNY TIPPED HER DARK head critically, bobbing it in time to the tinny, barely audible beat from her headphones, then gave a nod and popped a pink gum bubble. "You look great."

"Thanks." Samantha smiled at the skinny black-clad reflection behind her in the mirror of Jack's studio dressing room. Great wasn't exactly the term she'd use, but she did look…different.

Jenny had slicked back her hair and gathered it into a scalp-stretching bun at her nape. She'd shaded Samantha's eyes and cheekbones in brown, to provide contrast in the black-and-white photo, and painted her lips dark red, cheerfully assuring her they'd look black on the print—which Samantha wasn't sure she liked the sound of. Her lashes had been cemented into long stiff sweeps with so much mascara they felt like little eyelid weights. A stripe of black liner extended from the outer corner of each eye, evoking the Egyptian princess look. Thankfully she was spared the full-body makeup after Jenny pronounced her skin tone perfect for the particular dining table Jack was after.

How flattering to know her skin made good furniture. At least he wasn't shooting a cracked-leather armchair series. And frankly, if she and Jack were going to go at it after this charade was over, she'd just as soon not be covered in goop. Though she could imagine a pretty fun time in the shower washing it off....

She leaned toward the mirror, pretending to examine her new look, nerves buzzing. Jack was just as sexy as she remembered, maybe even more. From the second he opened the door and his face had erupted into that dazzling, sweep-a-girl-off-her-feet smile, Samantha had been overcome by lust. He was perfect. Love 'em and leave 'em Jack. Just what the divorce recovery doctor ordered.

She hoped this photography stuff went really, really quickly.

The chemistry between them was extraordinary. When she'd been teasing him, right before she let him off the hook with the ceiling fan joke, he'd been way, way aroused. Which was nice because she had been, too, and still was, thank you very much. The feeling lingered, an uncompleted ache between her legs.

She hadn't been able to flirt like that in ages. When she tried it on Brendan toward the end of their marriage, in hopes of retrieving some spark of passion, he accused her of treating him like a stranger, of making him uncomfortable. Well geez, that was kind of the *point.* To reach back to the exciting days when they *had* been strangers. Now she wondered if Brendan had a fear of highly sexual women. A fear Mr. Butthead obviously didn't share.

Yum.

"Here's your outfit." Jennifer rummaged in a closet, humming along to her silent music, the sound thin and strange without the accompanying harmonies. "I'll go outside to talk to him while you put it on."

She came up with the "outfit" and handed it over. Samantha put out her hand in utter disbelief. At the bar the other night Jack had said she wouldn't be wearing many clothes.

She wouldn't be. The scraps of fabric barely covered her palm. "This is an outfit?"

Jenny giggled. "The idea is that you look nude, without actually having to be."

"I see." Samantha held up the thong panties, hooked over her index finger. "A fine line."

"Don't worry, he's seen everything. I'll be right back."

"Okay." She watched Jenny bounce out, then re-examined the approximately three-square inch "outfit." If this little piece of nothing didn't look good on her she'd scream. Sexy underwear always looked so sexy on the hanger. But several mortifying ventures into lingerie dressing rooms had convinced her they made most of the stuff for fat-free aliens.

She stepped into the flesh-colored thong and pulled it up, praying it wouldn't be tight and make her hips bulge out on either side of the elastic.

It didn't. In fact, it fit. And looked…ahem. Very nice. Except she wasn't wild about the thong part invading her butt. Did people really enjoy all-day wedgies?

She pulled the top on and exhaled in a silent whistle. Tiny. But way sexy. Two strips of fabric covered the center of each breast, barely wide enough to hide her nipples. A thin gold cord connected the scraps and hooked behind her back, another ran halter-style around her neck.

A wicked smile spread over her face. If this wasn't a do-me outfit, she'd never seen one. All she needed was three-inch heels and a major attitude, and Jack would lose it. And did she *ever* need to make a man lose it.

A knock came on the door and Jenny's dark head peeked in, still bobbing to her soundless beat. "Samantha? Hey, you look great. But you need to take your necklace off."

Samantha's hand flew to her throat. She'd promised Brendan never to take it off. But then she'd also promised to stay married until death.

She took the necklace off, and laid it carefully on the counter, fingers back at her throat where its familiar weight wasn't anymore.

"He's ready for you."

"Okay." Samantha straightened her shoulders, lengthened her spine, and turned away from the necklace. She sure as hell was ready for him.

But first, she had to be a dining table.

She followed Jenny into the large warehouse studio, which managed to be colorful and intimate, divided into separate areas with tables and equipment, and an attractive arrangement of what must be often-used sets and props—including, she was most interested to note—a bed. She really hoped this shoot would go fast. She felt like an asteroid wanting impact with a heavenly body before she burned up in the atmosphere.

Jack stood with his back to her, bent over a camera in front of a white, curved wall at the opposite corner of the room, lit by an assortment of lamps at differing heights. She walked toward him…no, *prowled* toward him…excitement mounting, feeling like a sexual offering, arms swinging gracefully, her bare feet making next to no noise on the chilly floor. She couldn't wait to see his face. If the chemistry had sizzled when she still had clothes on, it ought to resemble a nuclear blast now.

This was so fun!

She stopped a few feet away and posed her body, pitched her voice down, husky and seductive. "I'm ready."

He straightened, and for a strange second she thought he'd hurt his back because he stayed there, frozen and stiff. Then he turned, jaw set, serious eyes in total contrast to the lazy laughing brown they'd been earlier.

He looked her over, inch by not-very-covered inch, as if she was a board at his local hardware store. What the heck had happened to him?

"Good job as usual, Jenny, thanks. We'll yell if we need you."

"'Kay." Jenny gave Samantha a thumbs-up and boogied back to the dressing room. Jack turned back to his camera.

Samantha's seductive smile froze solid on her face. She imagined it dropping off to shatter on the floor, along with her recently boosted self-esteem. O-kay. This was fine. No problem. Humiliation was her friend.

Apparently Jack took the make-her-into furniture thing very seriously. He just *better* be planning to make her into something more along the lines of sweaty and exhausted afterward. She didn't strut around half-naked with spandex wedged up her butt for nothing.

"Okay." Jack turned around again with an irritatingly impersonal smile that made her want to slug him. "Come over here."

She followed him, arms crossed over her chest, her feet thudding on the slanted painted-wood base of the curved wall.

"I'd like you right here, on your hands and knees, hands on this set of tape marks, knees on the other." He pointed to pieces of tape stuck to the white surface.

"Okay." Samantha knelt on the "knee" tape marks, thinking a stroll across hot coals sounded pretty terrific right about now.

Whatever had happened to produce this version of Jack, she hoped she got the other guy back after the shoot was over. She glanced up at him, squinting in the bright light. He towered over her, standing like a scowling brick wall with his hands on his hips. If he would just take a few steps closer, she could be hav-

ing a lot more fun on her knees than she was now—
and put a happy smile on his face in the bargain.

"Hands here." The hint of impatience in his voice
made her grit her teeth and extend her body, hands
in their appointed spot.

He stepped back behind his camera and examined
her.

Samantha held still, arching her back a little and
holding her stomach up so it wouldn't pooch down,
so she'd look stretched and lithe. He was probably
noticing her cellulite and the mole on her thigh and
the scar on her calf from when she took her brothers
up on a skateboarding dare. He was probably groaning, thinking how he'd have to airbrush it all out, use
some computer program to slenderize the line from
her butt to her thighs, basically change her entire—

"Perf—" The syllable came out husky and caught
in his throat, which he cleared loudly. "Perfect."

She turned to peek at him. Was that an erotically
induced speech impediment or an everyday frog in
his throat? He strode over to a nearby table, picked
up a clear plastic board with two formal table settings
glued to it and strode back, brow creased in a frown,
movements deft and purposeful, not at all like his
usual lazy swagger.

"This sits on your back. Can you get your spine a
little straighter? Lift here." He touched the small of
her back, a brief impersonal tap.

She lifted her back and felt the cool weight of the
tray, not as heavy as she'd expected.

"How does that feel?"

"Very…table-y."

"Good." He went back behind the lens and looked again, then adjusted the level of the tall lamp to his right. "Okay, now I want you to become a piece of furniture. Right now you still look like a woman."

She shot him a look. "I am a woman, Jack."

"Trust me, I know." His eyes softened, then as if he'd let something slip by him, he hardened them again. "But in this shot you're not a woman, you're a table. I want your face completely expressionless, I want your body like wood. Okay? Try it."

"Okay." Samantha's seductive smile jumped off the floor where it had lain in pieces all this time and glued itself back onto her face. *Trust me, I know*. If that look and that line were anything to go by, her Man To Do adventure was merely on hold. Get this shot right, get it out of the way and she'd be on to bigger and better adventures—where Jack was the one that needed to be woody.

At least two rolls of film, three lighting adjustments and an eternity later, her knees hurt, her back ached, and Mr. Perfectionist Photographer still hadn't gotten whatever the hell it was he wanted. Not to mention the small fact that she hadn't gotten what *she* wanted.

"Your back is sagging."

She glared straight ahead, still holding the pose. "My *boobs* will be sagging by the time this is over."

He peered at her over the top of his camera. "Need a break?"

"No." She straightened her spine. "Let's get it done."

"Can you bring your hips more into alignment?"

She rearranged her hips, taking the opportunity to ease the pressure on her knees. The tray was hitting her back in an odd place, and it had started to feel as if it was made of cement.

"Curl your pelvis under?"

She curled.

"Not quite." He came out from behind the camera and approached her. "I'll show you."

Samantha held her breath. Her extremely female parts sensed him behind her, his body close at her most vulnerable juncture. The lights had heated her skin and she could feel the cool of his shadow across her thighs. His hands locked onto her hips and she imagined them guiding her back, preparing her to feel him thrusting inside her.

"There." He gripped her steady. "Like that."

"Yes, I do."

For a second his hands lingered. She reacted with a surge of adrenaline, wanting him to stroke her bare skin, make slow circles leading inward until his thumbs came together and he could drag them up and down the slender strip of the thong, feel her soft flesh under the fabric, feel the moisture of her readiness.

Instead, his hands left cold spots on her sides as he walked back to his damn camera, obviously planning to ignore her. She didn't care. He wanted her and he sure as hell knew by now she wanted him, even if he hadn't seen the wet spot on her thong.

The camera clicked a few times. "Better, but I'm still not getting wood."

"Have you tried stroking it?"

He gave a frustrated groan that nearly made her giggle and blow her deadpan nonchalance. "Samantha…"

"Just trying to lighten things up."

"I'd rather they stayed heavy. And G-rated."

"*That's* no fun."

"Hold still. Think table." The camera clicked. "More."

Samantha rolled her eyes. "Has it ever occurred to you I'm simply a failure as furniture?"

"You have exactly what I want. I just have to find a way to get at it." He jerked his head up from behind the lens. "Don't even *touch* that one."

Samantha laughed. "Am I that bad?"

"Yes." He ducked back behind the camera. "You're that good. Now try again. Face still, eyes dead, body stiff."

Samantha clenched her jaw, glazed her eyes, made her body rigid. The camera clicked. God he was sexy. In some ways even sexier now, without his swaggering butthead routine going, when he was intense and focused like this, struggling to avoid the sexual pull between them, serious and intent on his work. She didn't know squat about photography, but by the size of his studio, the awards and portfolio prints covering the walls, and the intensity with which he worked, she'd guess she was in the presence of real talent. Which was always an aphrodisiac.

As if she needed any more of one.

"Samantha." His voice came out an exasperated growl. "What are you thinking about?"

"Sex."

He groaned and grabbed his hair with one hand. "There's the problem. Don't think about sex. Think about—"

"I know, I know. Furniture. But not beds."

"Right. Not beds. Think about how you'd feel if someone froze you in ice."

"Okay. Ice." She tried. She imagined herself cold, immobile, locked into a glacier somewhere, without sex for all eternity. The camera clicked. Until some well-muscled archeologist who looked strangely like Jack stumbled across her and thawed her out for some serious—

"You're doing it again."

"*What* am I doing again?"

"You have that light in your eye, that gleam. Get it off. Pretend you're stupid, that you haven't a single thought in your head. Think vapid, think idiot, think vacuum."

"Okay."

Nothing. She'd think about nothing. *Click.* Well she couldn't really think about nothing, but she certainly wouldn't think about the fact that she'd soon be having sex with Jack on the bed against the wall behind her. He must look absolutely amazing naked. He was the perfect size, broad without being body-builder fake. If the glance she'd gotten was anything to go by, his—

"Sa-man-*tha.*"

Oops.

"Okay, okay, I'm doing it again. But it's hard to be eighty-five percent naked with you right there and not think about sex."

Her voice dropped at the end of the sentence at the exact moment her brain caught up with what her mouth was doing. A thrill ran through her. *You go, Samantha.*

She held exactly still, not moving, not breathing. Was he coming toward her? Staying away? Torn between the two options? The tension was killing her.

Click.

Oh, for crying out loud. She exhaled her disappointment. Still taking the damn pictures.

"…Okay, I'll check." Jenny's voice floated over to them. "Jack?"

Jack turned and nodded expectantly. Jenny had come out of the dressing room, holding a cell phone to her ear.

"They need help at Bradley's, the job got out of hand. You okay here without me?"

Samantha frowned at the slight panic on Jack's face. What was *up* with the guy? Why didn't he jump at the chance to be alone with her?

"No problem." He smiled stiffly. "Thanks for the great job here. We're almost done."

"Okay. Bye, Samantha." Jenny backed away, grinning. "You look very table-ish."

"Thanks." Samantha reassumed the now-hated pose and grimaced. Not table-ish enough apparently. But at least with Jenny out of the studio there was some hope they could feel more intimate. If he ever managed to get this picture taken.

"I want you to think about your ex-husband."

Samantha's body tensed. His camera clicked. Clicked again. And again.

She turned her head and shot him a vicious glare. "That was low."

"Wasn't it?"

"Did it accomplish what you wanted?"

"Almost. Closest yet. You're still not quite there."

Enough. Samantha reached and took the tray off her back, sat up on her heels.

He peered over his camera and frowned. "What are you doing?"

"Giving up. Moving on. Sparing my knees."

"You're so close, Samantha. You just have to squelch that last bit of femininity and really concentrate."

"I've squelched all the femininity I can squelch." She spread her arms wide, presenting herself. "Face it, I'm too much woman for you."

The distant whine of the elevator taking Jenny to the ground floor sounded suddenly close and invasive. One of the lights made a tiny popping noise.

The impersonal cover dropped off Jack's eyes. One hand went to his hip, one masculine brow lifted. "I'll have you know there's no such thing."

"Oh?" She swallowed. The lights blazed down. Her breathing rose high into her chest. *Oh, baby. Here we go.*

"Prove it."

She waited, arms still outstretched, offering her body. This had to be it. What swaggering butthead could resist a challenge like that?

Apparently this one.

Instead of sweeping forward, carrying her to the bed and making her scream in ecstasy which is what he was damn well *supposed* to do, Jack stayed where was as if he'd glued himself to his tripod. Confusion crept over his face. What did the guy need, a guide? *Sex for Dummies?*

He ran a hand over his face and shook his head. "That's not what we're here for."

"What?" She wanted to scream with frustration. What was he talking about? "It's sure as hell what *I'm* here for."

He came unglued from his spot, took a few steps forward, then stood watching her, hands fisted on his hips. "I'm sorry about that. It's not the impression I meant to convey."

Samantha narrowed her eyes. Okay, so she'd been married for a while, out of circulation for longer, but there was no way she'd misjudged his signals that badly. No one could be that out of practice. "Come on, Jack. You made it out like this was going to be some wild adventure. Come late, after my staff is gone, and don't wear much. What did you think I was going to expect?"

Muscles bulged and retracted in his jaw. She could imagine the whirl of thoughts going on under his dark thick hair. "It's professional suicide to sleep with models."

Samantha stood stiffly and stalked over to him. Stood too close and was gratified when he didn't move back. His eyes bore down into hers, dark, and unless she was totally mistaken, hungry. "I'm not a model. I'm just a chick you met in a bar."

"You're modeling for me, that makes you a model. My career is too important to take a chance with."

She looked around the studio as if there might be someone she could do a reality check with. "Who is going to know? Who am I going to tell?"

"I can't risk it."

Samantha put one hand to her hip and dropped her forehead into the other.

"Okay, let me get this straight. You can't sleep with me because I might tell someone and it might get around that you had consensual sex with an adult woman."

"With one of my models. I don't need that reputation."

"Okay." She tapped her finger against her forehead. "So how about this. I didn't do the shot the way you wanted. Fire me as a model. Then we can have sex."

He burst out laughing. "Samantha, you must win every case you argue."

"I'm not a trial lawyer, but thanks." She moved closer and tipped her head to look up at him coyly. "It's just that it's been a while for me, and you are very sexy, and I think we could have fun."

She put her hand forward until it made contact with his chest, and let it rest there.

He groaned. "I know we could have fun."

She spread and contracted her fingers over the smooth muscle under his skin in a miniversion of a caress. All he needed was gentle persuasion. He was more than halfway convinced. "So?"

"So you're splitting hairs with the 'fire me and it won't count approach.'"

"You're going to make me beg, aren't you."

"Begging is a bad idea."

"Why, because you'll give in?"

"No, because it makes it that much harder—"

"That's what I'm after."

"Samantha." He sounded as if he was strangling, which was all the permission she needed.

"Please." She knelt, letting her hand trail down his chest until it came to rest just above his fly. "Please."

His breath came in and out, harsh labored jets. She leaned forward slowly, stopped an inch from the bulge in his jeans. "Please."

His breath hissed out. She moved forward, pressed her lips to the bulge, moved her head back and forth to increase the pressure, turned her face sideways and rubbed her cheek up and down.

"Don't...do that."

"Why?" She turned again, opened her lips, and made gentle toothless bites down the length of his erection. Oh, did that feel good, even to her. To come into contact with something warm and hard and male, to feel his reaction to her feminine power, to know that he was a quarter-inch from the edge and that she was about to push him over.

"Stop." He reached down, pulled her up and leaned her against one of the pillars supporting the ceiling, gripping her shoulders.

She stared at him. "Are you serious?"

His eyes traveled down her body. Slowly, intimately, not at all like he was examining a board at the hardware store. When his gaze reached her feet, he left his head hanging down and closed his eyes as if he was fighting demons she hadn't realized she was unleashing.

"Yes. I'm serious."

"But why? I mean why not?"

He took his hands off her shoulders, still not meeting her eyes. "I told you. Sleeping with models could ruin my career."

She narrowed her eyes. Something was very weird here. "Did that happen to you?"

"Don't ask."

"But I'm not like that."

"Samantha, this is my rule." He looked up and smiled grimly. "I am asking you to respect it."

"Of course," she whispered. "I'm sorry."

"I flirted with you in the bar because I was—because I *am* attracted to you. But I asked you to come here because I wanted you to do the shot. That's all I can give you."

"I see." The disappointment hit. Samantha closed her eyes, horrified to feel tears pricking. Of all the Swaggering Buttheads in the world, she had to pick a monk of one, with values. She looked around wildly, eyes unnaturally wide to keep the tears from spilling. "Where are my clothes?"

"Samantha." He took her shoulders again, not in anger this time, and looked earnestly into her face. "I'm really sorry."

"It's okay." She tried to pull away but he held her tightly and the tears she couldn't help spilled over onto her cheeks. She squeezed her lids shut. *Okay, Samantha, regroup.* Whatever impression he'd given in the bar, whatever anger and embarrassment she was feeling now over his rejection, blubbering wouldn't help anything. She owed herself and her pride a graceful dignified exit.

"I'm sorry." He whispered the words again and they came out with such tenderness that she opened her eyes and stared into his. God they were beautiful. Dark and expressive and full of life and pain. She felt an intense connection, a pull that went right inside her and surprised the hell out of her.

He leaned forward slowly and kissed her. She closed her eyes again, disappeared into the soft comforting feel of his warm mouth on hers. Ohhh, it felt good to be kissed again. More than that, the gentle contact made her crying stop. Made her feel safe and strangely elated and no longer quite so confused and rejected.

He pulled back and smiled, a nice-guy caring smile. "You okay?"

"Yes." She wiped at her tears, probably smudging the hell out of her makeup. "Are you?"

He laughed. "Yeah. Blue balls and I have become friends."

She giggled and sniffed a few times into the silence, feeling she had to say something, but no idea what.

"So…you're not having sex at *all?*" The question was absurd but she simply couldn't comprehend the waste.

"Not randomly. And not recently. No."

"Okay…well…thank you." The words came out breathless and silly. He probably had no idea what she was thanking him for since he couldn't tell what a rescue his kiss had performed on the downward spiraling of her mood. "For being…gentle about it."

"You're welcome." He released her and stepped back. "Please believe it's not that I don't want to."

"Okay." She wrapped her arms around herself, still feeling off-balance and not at all sure she wouldn't cry again. "I better go get dressed."

Back in the dressing room she hauled off the flimsy outfit, washed her face clean, put her necklace and earrings back on, and changed into her outfit, the one she'd bought with so much hope and excitement. Right now she couldn't wait to go home and put on cutoffs and her ugly fuzzy pink slippers.

Ostensibly, her first Man To Do adventure had been a disaster. She had her lips pressed to his erection, which would make any guy turn into Org the Cave Man, and he'd said no, firmly and without looking back. Total humiliation.

And yet, it didn't feel quite that way. His kiss had

given her ballast, steadied her emotions, which had been in danger of whipping themselves up into a regular typhoon of misery.

In a weird way that kiss had been almost more intimate than the anonymous hot sex she'd counted on. It had certainly touched her more deeply. Maybe she would rethink her belief—or current lack thereof—in Fate. Maybe that's what she'd been sent here for. One taste of intimacy just to reassure her that intimacy was waiting for her when she chose to be ready again.

She winced at her bedraggled reflection in the mirror, then tried out a smile which improved things considerably. So Jack was out, for now anyway, damn shame too, though she'd try not to linger on that aspect.

Which meant her Man To Do was still at large here in Chicago, waiting to be done.

It was just a question of finding him.

6

From: Samantha Tyler
Sent: Friday
To: Erin Thatcher; Tess Norton
Subject: The Big Event

Well. Last night wasn't quite what I expected. To start with—deep breath—we didn't have sex.

I know, I know. You're both screaming, "What?" Well, it turns out he won't sleep with his models (Samantha rolls eyes at ceiling). Just my luck. You guys find Men To Do on the first try that turn out to be the loves of your lives and I can't even get laid (grinning away).

But here's the really weird part. I don't mind. I can't even begin to explain why I don't feel rejected and miserable. But I don't. I did at first, when I realized he was serious about staying away, but then in an entirely un-Swaggering Butthead fashion, he was so torn up about it, and when he saw how torn up I was, he kissed me in this totally sweet nonsexual way and the rest of it suddenly didn't matter so much.

I feel calmer and more peaceful than I have in a

long time. Jack wasn't my Man To Do, but I know mine is out there and I'm definitely ready to find him! What's more—and I think this is what last night did for me that sex wouldn't have—for the first time I am allowing a little ray of hope to creep back in that someday I really will find someone I can be with forever.

Go figure.

Samantha

P.S. I made an absolutely lousy dining table.

Samantha finished answering and sending other e-mail that actually had something to do with her work, then swiveled back to her paper- and file-strewn desk. She'd been making headway on a number of cases recently, gotten one horrific racist fired, another misogynist slapped down. Life was good.

Her curiously elated mood had grown after last night's adventure. The day seemed brighter, trees seemed greener, people around her didn't even seem as snarly and surly as usual. How grim she must have been for so long, without even realizing it, until she'd been launched into this unexpected happy plateau.

Of course she did feel wistful once in a while. The kind of chemistry she'd had with Jack didn't come along every day. And she had been looking forward to some skin-to-skin contact, she still needed that. If it wasn't for the sense of closure when she left him, and the relative peace she'd found since then, she might wish she could see him again. But the evening had built and waned like the sex act itself, with their banter in his reception area as foreplay, the table shoot as the sex with the climax of her tears and his kiss, and now the lovely satisfying afterglow.

To call him again would be to sully that beautiful act, disorder the perfect emotional sequence, and risk putting her and Jack back into the mire of confusion and uncertain misunderstanding they'd fought their way out of.

Maybe someday. Not now. She'd always remember him fondly as The Man Who Gave Her Hope. From now on, her life would go better. A few sexual escapades and then the search for something more lasting. Jack had been the gateway to her future.

Samantha pushed her hair back in frustration. God, it all sounded so sane. Like a chapter out of one of her feel-good surviving-divorce books. If only she could be sure it was true. She'd been up and down so many times over the last year or two she had no idea what was what anymore.

"Samantha?" Lyssa knocked, poking her unsmiling face around the door to peek into the office.

Samantha didn't even try to look busy. "Yes, Ms. Lyssa?"

"I set up your appointment with Tanya Banyon for next Thursday. Here's the file from the Dixon case. Need me for anything else? If not I'm off to lunch." Lyssa tossed the file onto Samantha's desk and stood waiting, hands fisted on her stunning aqua suit, mouth a tight line.

Samantha narrowed her eyes. "What's wrong?"

Lyssa's face threatened to crumple. "Is it that obvious?"

"Um…yes."

"Bill." She inhaled and exhaled sharply. "He has informed me that it would be good for both of us to see other people."

"Oh, Lyssa." Samantha's stomach clenched in sympathy. Lyssa got dumped practically every other month. Mostly because she insisted on being attracted to idiots who didn't appreciate her. She gestured to the chair in front of her desk. "Sit and spill. What do you think it means?"

"It means he met Alexa, Ms. Perfection, and wants to be able to screw her while I continue to provide him with friendship and emotional support."

"Oh, God." Samantha made the same face she made when she tasted brussel sprouts. "*What* a charmer."

"Yeah, well, you know what?" Lyssa smacked her palms on the arms of her chair. "I'm sick of rejection. I'm not taking this one lying down."

Samantha smacked her desk in a show of female unity. "Atta girl."

"I'm betting he won't think it's such a good idea if I find my own male version of Alexa Perfection."

"I'm betting you're right. Way to go, Lyssa."

Lyssa slumped down into her chair. "Only trouble is, I don't know any male Alexas. The woman is one of those mysterious pouty smoldering types."

"Not that you're exactly hideous yourself."

"But I have the wholesome girl-next-door thing

going. This woman looks like she can screw six guys at once and not spill a drop of her citron vodka martini.'' She leaned back, then turned toward Samantha without lifting her head from the chair. ''You know any gorgeous guys I can go out with to piss him off?''

Jack. Samantha's body went rigid. Jack was perfect. Jack was gorgeous. Lyssa was gorgeous. Lyssa wasn't his model. Jack wouldn't have to hold back. Bill would get jealous. Lyssa would feel better. Samantha would have helped a friend. Jack would probably be totally into it.

Jack.

She instructed her mouth to say it. J-a-c-k. The man she'd gone beyond but would always remember fondly. The one she didn't want to call because it would spoil their night, violate the closure. The one who was her gateway to the future. Who she was over. And didn't mind not seeing again. Jack. *Jack. Say it, Samantha.*

A wave of violent jealousy shocked her. Oh. My. Goodness. Her capacity to shovel the bull all over herself was amazing. How could she be this selfish? Jack was just what Lyssa needed, Samantha had just finished telling herself she was over the entire episode, that Jack had been good for her precisely in that limited capacity, and suddenly there was no way in hell Samantha was giving him up. How could she fool herself so completely? *Help.*

''Samantha?'' Lyssa was staring at what must be a frozen look of panicked horror on Samantha's face.

''Um…I was just thinking about whether you

would like…'' Her mind grasped for anything remotely reasonable—other than Jack. "…my ex-husband.''

"Brendan?'' Lyssa sat up straight. "Wow. I mean, you wouldn't mind? Just for lunch. Would he do it?''

"I think he'd love it. He thinks you're terrific. He'd be perfect.'' Samantha smiled, feeling as though she was baring her teeth, and dashed Brendan's work number onto a card to hand to Lyssa. How could she have been so blind? How could she think Jack was nothing but a stepping-stone one minute, be more than ready to move on, and the next minute have to keep from scratching Lyssa's eyes out at the mere thought of them together? For lunch!

What happened to peace? What happened to stability? When would these little islands of calm in her life turn into a substantial mainland? An entire continent, even? Was being in control of her own brain really so much to ask?

"Cool.'' Lyssa took the card and glanced at it, then frowned at Samantha. "You're sure you don't mind? You look a little green.''

"No, it's fine.'' Samantha managed a hearty chuckle. Better Lyssa thought she was having an ex-wife pang or two than know she was completely insane. "It felt weird for about a nanosecond, but I'm totally over it.''

"You won't change your mind and hate me?''

"No chance.'' Samantha came up with a real smile. "Call him. Brendan has all the credentials and he loves devious little plots. He's already your friend, so you'll be comfortable with him, and most of all, he'll make Bill crazy.''

''Excellent.'' Lyssa tapped the card on her palm. ''I'll call right now.''

Samantha held on to her smile until Lyssa was out of the room, then slumped back in her chair. Oh man. What the hell was she going to do now?

She straightened and shook her head. One thing she'd learned going through this divorce and being constantly swept in and out on varying tides of emotion, was never to make decisions at the peak of any mood. Give the tides a few days to settle and wait for a winner to emerge, a solution that felt right for more than a few hours.

Obviously she'd been in denial. She still had unresolved feelings where Jack was concerned. Maybe she wasn't quite over her disappointment that things hadn't worked out and a little more grieving would take care of it. Maybe she was fixating on him because he was the first attractive man to catch her eye in a long time and she needed to believe that he wouldn't be the last. That all made pretty good sense.

The problem was, in the hot humid light of morning, having spent entirely too much awake time during the night going over and over the evening with Jack, she couldn't get rid of the feeling that he'd been using the model thing as an excuse. Or that there was at very least something more to it which he hadn't felt he could tell her.

She rolled her eyes. Brendan had been charming and glib, but when it came to real emotional sharing, nope, nothing, *nada*. A hot button for her, that was all. She couldn't expect Jack to spill his every private emotion to a stranger.

She shoved back from her desk and grabbed her purse. Lunchtime. She needed to get out of here. She'd go to the specialty food store nearby where she usually went, and grab something to eat at her desk.

Inside the store, after she'd ordered a sandwich from the deli, the produce aisle beckoned. She was suddenly heartily sick of frozen food for dinner every night. Her body was absolutely craving something nonprocessed. Like a huge salad.

She lugged her basket over and chose some beautiful fresh lettuce, arugula, scallions, and paused with her hand over the Belgian endive. Someone was behind her. She could feel his expectation.

"The tomatoes are delicious. I got some here last week."

Samantha spun around and looked into the chest and then up into the face of Rick Grindle, offering a handful of perfect scarlet tomatoes.

"Oh." She held out her basket and he dropped two inside. "Thank you."

"Needed to get out?"

She shot a look up at his face. "I'm sorry?"

"Of the office." He gestured around him. "Sometimes a change of scene helps. I had a difficult morning myself. Coming here, seeing the good things the earth can produce, helps stabilize me."

"Oh...yes." She felt an eerie sense of disorientation, as she had in his office, as if he was somehow able to tap into her thoughts. "It's nice to get away. I'm sorry you were having a difficult morning, too."

He grimaced and shrugged his huge shoulders. "As you can imagine, the accusations in the office have produced unpleasant repercussions. I try to ignore it and do my job, but it can get to me occasionally."

"I can imagine." She braced herself for more self-defense. More protestations of his innocence. How he was being hounded and suspected his career would be ruined by the mere rumor of impropriety.

"They make oregano and sun-dried tomato feta that would be fabulous in your salad. And there are some very nice Kalamata olives in the display over there."

"Thanks. That does sound good." She glanced into his basket. Chicken breasts. Prosciutto. Anchovy paste. Pasta. Artichokes. "Do you cook?"

"Yes. It's relaxing and therapeutic. On my tensest days I generally eat the best. How about you?"

"Not usually. Cooking for one is sort of depressing."

"Only if you look at it that way, Samantha." His deep voice lightened a bit, became gentle, persuasive. "Try it tonight. Have a glass of wine while you prepare your meal. Play music, nothing jarring. You'll feel more relaxed, more like yourself." He smiled and moved closer to avoid someone walking behind him in the narrow aisle. "Trust me."

She stared into his gray eyes, enjoying a mental imagine of herself dining on a sumptuous meal in her apartment instead of sucking down prefabricated mass-produced salt-laden flavorless garbage. The idea immediately appealed.

"Thanks, Rick." She smiled at him, genuinely touched at his concern for her emotional state. For some reason, even coming from a stranger, it made her feel less alone, less confused. "I think I'll try it."

JACK LAY ON HIS queen-sized bed, with the cherry frame his father had made for him, one hand under his head, the other holding the contact sheet displaying the shots he took of Samantha last night. It was just before midnight after an absolute ball-buster of a day in the studio. Nothing had gone smoothly, everything was due. He was exhausted.

And he couldn't take his eyes off her.

His instinct had been right on. The camera loved her. His other instinct was right on also. He hadn't been able to get a good table shot.

He dropped the arm holding the contact sheet and stared at the ceiling, where a small spider was making itself at home. The pictures he'd gotten so far—the chair, the coatrack, the ottoman, were all perfect. Four models who had so completely erased their humanity that they could have been posed mannequins.

Not Samantha. He couldn't suppress her no matter what he did. Even when she was holding absolutely still, her body burst with vitality and sensuality. Even doing her best table impersonation, she looked like a centerfold.

And forget suppressing the emotion in her eyes.

He sat up, still holding the contact sheet and swung

his legs over the edge of the bed. What was he going to do? About the pictures? About the series? About her? Should he forget photographing her and give her what she wanted? Forget the sex and keep photographing her? Forget her completely?

The hardest part about the evening hadn't been keeping himself from her physically, though when she'd had her open lips on his fly, he'd nearly done a cock-for-brain exchange. He still had lipstick marks on those jeans and was tempted, like a lovestruck teenage rockstar fan, never to wash them again.

He grinned and rubbed the aching muscles at the back of his neck. The hardest part had been when he realized how much he wanted to explain. To tell her why he wouldn't let himself sleep with her. Other women he'd turned down with a simple no and to hell with what they thought.

But this one, standing there in an outfit that would turn a gay man straight, with mirror-of-her-soul eyes and welling tears, he'd wanted *her* to *understand* why. He'd wanted to tell her more. About Krista. About the hell he'd been through. Yet all he'd been able to do was kiss her, with more tenderness than desire, battle an overwhelming urge to hold her and make her world okay.

Maria was right. The woman was a splinter. With a barbed point.

He got to his feet, crossed the plank flooring to the kitchen, grabbed a beer and went back into his room, laying the contact sheet on the desk, straightening another pile of papers that had been knocked askew. He turned on his lamp and opened the drawer to his right, located his loupe in the close corner where he could reach it easily, and put it on the most promising picture of Samantha, the only one marked with grease pencil; the one where he'd told her to think about her ex-husband.

Dirty trick, but she'd responded immediately by freezing exactly the way he'd been trying to get her to all evening. He bent over the frame and studied it through the magnifying lens. Body perfect, expression all wrong. Surprise and pain, shock and anger, the woman couldn't hide a thing she felt. She was magnificent in two dimensions. Probably the most magnetic model he'd ever seen.

Jack narrowed his eyes, staring at the picture, a hazy idea taking shape in the back of his mind. She wasn't right for the furniture series. But a face and body like that cried out to be captured on film, in a way that would suit who she was.

He jerked his head up from the loupe. He wanted to photograph her again. A series of nudes. Black and white, more shadow than light, where she could allow her sensuality and emotions to break through.

The chair creaked as he pushed back from his desk, grabbed his beer and stalked into his living room. The images jumped into his head as if he'd already taken the pictures. Samantha lying on her back, body curved as if she was draped over a giant ball, light from the right to leave half her body in shadow, one breast exposed the other dark, the fabulous long curve of her hip delineated in soft black and soft white. Half anonymous, half exposed.

He took a long swig of Leinenkugel's Northwoods Lager. Then another. The ideas kept coming, spilling over him and he paced back and forth on his Oriental rug, to the big screen TV, to the bookcase. Over and back, over and back, accompanied by Samantha. Facing away from the camera now, looking back over her shoulder toward the viewer, not at him, never quite at him, her face in shadow but not deeply, so the expression in her eyes would come out. A woman essentially frozen, essentially posed, but the femininity, the sexuality that she couldn't suppress capturing the viewer.

Fabulous. Perfect. The new pictures would complement and contrast with his furniture series, make the show at the New Eyes Gallery more substantial.

Jack stopped pacing. And he'd be an entry in the *Guiness Book of Records* for the world's longest erection.

Shit.

He was going to have to have a talk with himself about this. Either reevaluate his philosophy and make an exception in Samantha's case, or prepare himself for agony.

Back into his bedroom, he dropped the loupe over another picture, and stared at this fascinating woman with the killer body and vulnerable eyes. He let himself look as a man this time, not a photographer.

Her body was long, her breasts small and rounded. Her arms were slender and strong-looking. Her rear curved deliciously, an invitation for the eye to go on a sliding trip down the firm lines of her thighs.

He hardened immediately and groaned, remembering the view when he'd stood behind her to adjust her hips. That tiny strip of fabric, clinging to her sex, her legs slightly spread. How he ever managed to walk away he hadn't a clue. He'd wanted to press his face to the fabric of the thong, inhale her scent, drive her crazy with his tongue, slide his hands up and around the perfect smooth skin of her hips.

Why the hell hadn't he? Why did all his noble reasoning sound like so much cowardly crap right now? After all, this woman wasn't Krista. Krista ate women like this for a snack. Nor was Samantha in the photography or modeling business, which meant she wasn't likely to let their liaison slip to anyone who knew him. And his feelings toward her, that unfamiliar tenderness and even more unfamiliar intimacy were indications that he wasn't going to be in this just to get lucky, and piss her off by dumping her the next morning. This wasn't a woman he'd get enough of in one night.

He lifted his head and considered his neat assortment of sharpened pencils. Who was to say she wouldn't get bored of *him* after one night?

She'd said she was looking for fun. Mr. Right Now instead of Mr. Right. Someone like that wouldn't be angry when the affair ended. She'd be free to get her life back on track.

Right? *Right?*

Yeah, right.

He rolled his eyes and reached for his beer. His reasoning had gone south the second his dick got hard. Men were such noble creatures.

The truth of the matter was, he was crazy to photograph her. And even crazier to sleep with her. On the latter point he still had a few issues to work out. On the former, there were none. The idea for the new series with Samantha had sprung fully formed out of his head, like Athena out of Zeus's. So at least one decision he'd go with, the one his brain had been involved in making.

He'd call her first thing in the morning.

THE WOMAN—MARCY WAS IT?—writhed, her body broke out into a sweat. She was close. Rick reacted immediately, stopped the teasing flicks with his tongue, clamped his lips firmly over her clit and sucked hard.

"Oh!" She let out a screech and came wildly. Her third. He watched her shudder and moan with detached satisfaction. They always came easily with him. He knew women. He knew what they liked. He listened to them, that's all they really wanted, all men really had to do. Listen to their words and listen to their bodies.

But three orgasms was plenty for her now. It was his turn. He rose onto his arms over her.

"Johnny." She smiled at him, luminous, dreamy, and trailed her hands up the biceps and triceps he worked hard to keep impressive. "That was amazing."

He kissed her, working her patiently with his lips and tongue. She was a pretty lousy kisser. Loose-lipped. But the idea of her tasting her own juice from his mouth turned him on.

He drew his tongue from her mouth, laved it over her neck, over the scarlet dog collar he had her wear, down to her breast implants, like a mama cat washing her young. Her body was too bony for his taste; the line of her collarbone was sunken, not proud. But once he was inside her, he could close his eyes and pretend she was Samantha. Lose himself in the tight clasp of a female pussy and dream.

He smiled at her and reached for the box of condoms he kept next to his nightstand. He wouldn't need one with Samantha. She was clean. He'd hacked into her doctor's file just to be sure. And he'd kept himself clean, wearing condoms with every woman he'd been with since age sixteen.

"Put it on for me." He sat on the bed, his cock huge and hard while Marcy rolled the condom on him. He liked having to buy the large size. Women liked it, too. Whoever said size didn't matter had a pencil-dicked husband she was trying to make feel better.

"Turn over. On your hands and knees."

She turned over obediently, her too-small ass sticking in the air. He shoved inside her and started pumping hard. This woman liked it rough. Good thing. He was in the mood for the rough stuff. He closed his eyes and transformed her skinny too-gangly body into

Samantha's slender tight one. His body responded with a wave of arousal and he pumped harder.

Samantha had been thinking about sex the entire time she'd been in his office. He'd had the fight of his life to maintain his calm, to concentrate on his performance. He'd fooled her completely, turned the tables on Tanya. And he'd gotten to her just as he planned. Her lips had gone from tight to luscious, her skin had flushed. He could practically smell the confusion, the tinge of sexual awareness. At noon, too, in the grocery store where he'd followed her, she had been uncomfortable, aroused, stared at him like he was her savior.

He imagined her at her dinner, sipping wine, listening to music as he'd told her to do, thinking of him and getting wet, maybe without noticing or realizing where her pleasure came from.

His thrusting became a frenzy, Marcy's head banged against the headboard in a sex-rhythm that excited him further. He groped for her ass, eyes still closed, and gave her a series of hard slaps. She loved that stuff, the humiliation. Samantha wouldn't at first, but eventually he knew she'd come around. He'd have to get to that point slowly with her. He never forced women. Just led them into what they didn't know they wanted until he showed them how much they did.

Samantha would be a volcano in bed. She'd love sex of all kinds, rough, tender, sweet, savage, every way he knew how to give it to her, or she to him. He knew it as surely as he knew he was about to come all over this woman he was with now. Just thinking about the heat he and Samantha would generate, just thinking about that, about her ass, her tits, her...

"Turn over."

He shoved Marcy off him, twisted her onto her back, pulled off the condom and worked his cock until he spurted all over her eager face and chest. She loved that stuff, this woman.

Samantha would love it more.

His next move would come soon, before she got more involved with this Jack character. The fascination with Jack was starting to irritate him. He'd have to plan more calls for Johnny Orion, to keep her sexual interest high. More encounters with Rick—though not too soon so as not to arouse her suspicion—to nurture the intimacy he'd planted already. After that it was only a matter of time until he connected the dots. Johnny Orion and Rick Grindle. Everything a woman could want in one package.

Jack Hunter didn't stand a chance.

7

From: Erin Thatcher
Sent: Thursday
To: Samantha Tyler; Tess Norton
Subject: re: The Big Event

Well. Hmm. I'm not quite sure I know what to say. Didn't we originally decide our Man To Do pact was about sex, sex and more sex? Yep. I'm pretty damn sure that was our deal. Which means it's time for you to pay up, girlfriend. Not having sex, indeed! <grin>

Still, the night does sound intriguing. And the fact that YOU are feeling better about things and about relationships and about yourself... I'd have to say you did the right thing. Besides, you never know what might happen with the SB further down the road. (Swaggering Butthead—that still cracks me up!) Especially if you realize that you are not meant to be a dining table. <grin> You are definitely a Victorian period settee!

Now, about that kiss...<evil grin> Let's hear a few details!

Love, Erin

From: Tess Norton
Sent: Friday
To: Samantha Tyler; Erin Thatcher
Subject: re: The Big Event

Oh, honey, you got me all teary. I do want you to believe love is possible, cause if you don't believe it (sort of like Tinkerbell) it won't happen for you. I'm clapping my hands. I believe enough for two, so I'm cutting you a little slack, but only for a tiny little while. Whatever you have to do to nurture this thought, do it. See wildly romantic movies. Read romance novels and plenty of them. Listen to your own heart, and trust your deepest instincts.

So, uh, may I ask how long you intend to be his model? Does his non-screwing of models have a statute of limitations? Can you quit being his model right this second?

I think you should continue to look for another Man To Do, but under no circumstances stop this whatever the hell it is with your SB. I like him. A man with ethics. Wow. Who'da thunk?

You deserve love and happiness. Let yourself be open to it.

Mahatma Tess has spoken

P.S.—Dining table. Hmm. Somehow I don't think it's a negative that you didn't excel at being one.

Samantha twisted her mouth to one side then the other. The girls didn't get it. But then they had both found true love recently so that's all they could see. From their perspective, men were either good for sex

Play the
Romance Crossword Game

and get...
2 FREE BOOKS

and a
FREE GIFT...

YOURS to KEEP!

Scratch Here!

to reveal the hidden words.
Look below to see what you get.

Yes!

I have scratched off the gold areas. Please send me my **2 FREE BOOKS** and **FREE GIFT** for which I qualify. I understand that I am under no obligation to purchase any books as explained on the back of this card.

▼ DETACH AND MAIL CARD TODAY! ▼

350 HDL DRT5   150 HDL DRUM

FIRST NAME   LAST NAME

ADDRESS

APT.#   CITY

STATE/PROV.   ZIP/POSTAL CODE

Visit us online at
www.eHarlequin.com

ROMANCE	MYSTERY	NOVEL	GIFT
You get **2 FREE BOOKS** PLUS a **FREE GIFT!**	You get **2 FREE BOOKS!**	You get **1 FREE BOOK!**	You get a **FREE MYSTERY GIFT!**

Offer limited to one per household and not valid to current Harlequin Blaze™ subscribers.
All orders subject to approval.

© 2001 HARLEQUIN ENTERPRISES LTD. ® and ™ are trademarks owned by Harlequin Enterprises Ltd.   (H-B-02/03)

The Harlequin Reader Service® — Here's how it works:

Accepting your 2 free books and mystery gift places you under no obligation to buy anything. You may keep the books and gift and return the shipping statement marked "cancel." If you do not cancel, about a month later we'll send you 4 additional books and bill you just $3.80 each in the U.S., or $4.21 each in Canada, plus 25¢ shipping and handling per book and applicable taxes if any.* That's the complete price and — compared to cover prices of $4.50 each in the U.S. and $5.25 each in Canada — it's quite a bargain! You may cancel at any time, but if you choose to continue, every month we'll send you 4 more books, which you may either purchase at the discount price or return to us and cancel your subscription.

*Terms and prices subject to change without notice. Sales tax applicable in N.Y. Canadian residents will be charged applicable provincial taxes and GST. Credit or Debit balances in a customer's account(s) may be offset by any other outstanding balance owed by or to the customer or good for forever. They'd lost sight of the gray in-between where guys like Jack dwelt.

She wasn't into finding someone for a real relationship. There was so much to do and see now, so many men to check out, time where she could feel single and free and good about herself by herself. The parting kiss with Jack had opened a new chapter of her life. Just because the physical contact made her feel good didn't mean there was something magical about him. She could just as easily have felt that way if someone else had—

The intercom on her desk buzzed. "Samantha, there's a Jack Hunter here to see you."

Samantha's stomach took a sharp, breath-stealing dive. Here? Jack? Jack was *here?* She blew out a stress-breath, shoved her chair around from her computer, pushed her hair behind her ears, straightened her silk blouse, picked up a pen to look busy and pulled an open file closer. "Thanks, Lyssa. Send him in."

The door opened.

"Hi."

She raised her eyes from her file, intending to watch him saunter over with a cool, measuring look. Instead, a grin took over her face to match the one on his. Damn. One glimpse and all her noble thoughts about his over-and-done-with platonic role in her life went spinning out the window. He was here. He was male. He was hot. God help her.

"Jack. What a surprise."

He dropped into the chair in front of her desk, long

and lean and edibly good-looking, bringing in a hint of aftershave and male sweat from the summer outdoors. "A nice one?"

Samantha shrugged and prepared to deliver the understatement of the year. "Sure."

"Good." He relaxed back, elbows resting on the arms of the chair, regarding her with dark eyes and an amused smile.

Samantha raised one eyebrow, appearing way-cool while her insides were experiencing an earthquake. Why the hell was he here? Was he going to ask her to do more no-sex modeling? Or no-modeling sex? Or was he here to check up on her sanity as a friend? She couldn't let herself care. "So is this a social visit or a professional one?"

"Both." He sat up straight, away from the back of the chair. "I want to photograph you again."

She couldn't help a jolt of disappointment. Okay, so she cared. More modeling. No sex. "Not the damn table again."

He chuckled. "Something different. You are dynamite on film, Samantha."

"But not as furniture."

"Not as furniture."

"So what now, bathroom fixtures? Kitchen appliances?"

He leaned forward, arms resting on his thighs, eyes alight with the intensity that got to her in a way his sexy swagger didn't. "I want to do a series of nudes."

Samantha burst out into incredulous laughter. "You want me to take my clothes off."

"Yes."

"All of them."

"Yes."

He was staring at her now with mischief mixed into his intensity, and just the faintest hint of that hunger she'd glimpsed two nights ago in his studio.

Samantha squeezed her crossed thighs together. *Ohhh my.* Was she being invited professionally or seduced outright? Right now, with the incredible unexpected high of seeing him again, a high that pulverized all the comforting lies she'd been telling herself about her feelings toward him, either would be fine.

"Hmm." She swiveled her chair back and forth and touched her pen to the corner of her mouth. "Interesting idea."

Which she might be nuts enough to consider. The guy drew her in a powerful way that made her sound judgment and rational reasoning skills dysfunctional at the mere sight of him. How did he *do* that? More importantly, what horrible personal weakness made her let him?

His eyes dropped from hers to the pen touching her lips. Her body reacted to his gaze on her mouth as if he'd actually kissed her. In a sudden fit of boldness, she opened her lips and captured the tip of the pen inside.

His eyes shot back to hers. She kept swiveling. Back and forth, trying to drive him completely nuts for no sane reason except that sitting here opposite his magnetic masculinity, she desperately wanted to. Push that envelope. Feel alive again. Sexual. Feminine. Powerful. And the dark energy in his eyes was telling her that even if he didn't leap over the desk and do her right here among her files, he was imagining it.

"What do you think, Samantha?"

"I'm not sure I should tell you."

"Maybe you better not." He let his eyes linger on hers, for another lap-warming second, then pulled a sheet out of his file. "This is why I want to photograph you again."

He put the contact sheet on her desk and pointed to one of the pictures, marked in red crayon. Samantha leaned over it, careful to let her hair brush his arm. The image of her was stark and startling, rigid on her hands and knees with an expression of combined horror and distaste on her way-too-made-up face. "Whoa. I look like a jungle sacrifice."

"You're incredible."

She closed her eyes, just for a second, to let his words wash over her. Yes, it did her heart good to be called that, even if she couldn't quite agree given what the picture looked like to her. "So…now you want me naked."

"Yes, I do."

She raised her head from the bizarre sight of herself on film. He returned her look calmly, his expression not giving the answer she wanted, damn him. Was he mixing signals again? Promising sex with his eyes and attitude, then when she got to his studio, reverting to the consummate professional with nothing but photography on his mind? She wanted him, there was no question. But she wasn't incredibly excited at the prospect of facing rejection again.

"Jack."

"Yes."

"Is this just about taking pictures?"

He grinned, a slow grin that spread his sexy mouth wide, that sent reverberations down through her own body. "Of course, Samantha, what else would it be about?"

She had to suppress a laugh of sheer delight. When he was a Swaggering Butthead, he was a joy to be with. It was that other guy, the intense serious one that got her all confused, that she couldn't quite figure out how to deal with. "Did anyone ever tell you that you're a tease?"

He leaned in suddenly. Close enough so that she could almost kiss him just by lurching forward in her chair. "No."

"Jack?"

"Yes."

"You're a tease." She smiled sweetly. "There. Now someone has."

He chuckled, reached out and pushed her hair back behind her ears in a tender familiar gesture that made her want to jerk away and ask him to do it again all at the same time.

"So will you do it?"

"Well..." She repeated the motion his hand had

made, as if superimposing her gesture would erase his, keep her body safely hers. "On one condition."

"What's that?"

"After you're finished taking pictures of me naked?"

"Yes."

"I get to pick what we do."

"Samantha…"

She shrugged. "Seems fair to me."

He stood and walked around behind her desk, examined the John Marin prints she had on her wall. She swiveled her chair around to follow his movement.

"I'm the one who has to take her clothes off. It's only fair I get to choose one of the evening's activities."

Jack turned to her, jaw set, mouth grim, eyes dancing. "This is blackmail."

"Yes."

He sat on the low counter running along the back wall of her office, arms crossed over his chest, long legs stretched out. "You know I'm tempted."

"God, I hope so."

He laughed. "So I don't get your body just for art's sake?"

She smiled a smug smile and shook her head. God this was fun. How could she think she could write this man off as a sweet, gentle push into her future? If he'd waive his rule about models, which no matter what he said she had a feeling his showing up today indicated he would, Jack Hunter was the guy she wanted for her Man To Do. The tension between them was so powerful the actual sex might be an anti-climax.

Or not.

"No. You don't get my body just for your art."

"I'll tell you what." He rubbed his chin thought-fully. "You show up. I'll do the shoot. Then we can talk about what happens next."

"Ha!" She couldn't keep the smile off her lips, no matter how stern she tried to keep them. "You think I'll fall for that one?"

He grinned at her, a rueful boyish grin that did something vaguely nutty to her insides. She tilted her head and regarded him coyly. His smile faded; the heat flared in his eyes. Which did something much, much better than vaguely nutty. "Samantha."

"Yes." The word came out a hoarse whisper and she cleared her throat. "Yes."

"Is anyone likely to come into your office in the next few minutes?"

She bit her lip and reached for the necklace at her throat. "Why?"

"Answer first, then I'll tell you."

"No." She peeked over her shoulder at the door. Doubtful anyway. "Why?"

"Because." He got up from the counter and moved toward her, making her take in a sudden deep breath. "I don't want to be interrupted."

He stopped in front of her chair and looked down at her, hands on his hips.

She had to swallow to speak again. "Are we going to be doing something we don't want interrupted?"

He leaned forward, put his hands to her waist and lifted her so she was standing all of one inch away from him.

"Yes. We are."

She made a silly gasping sound and he kissed her, without hesitation or the slightest sense that he had anything but complete rights to her mouth.

Samantha clung to him, slid her arms up around his neck, pressed her body against him, giving herself over to the passionate, primal sensations. It had been so damn long.

His arms closed around her, held her tightly so that she practically cried with how sweet it was to be held, to be kissed, to be wanted like this.

He broke the kiss, released her body to hold her head between his hands, and ran his thumbs down her cheeks. "Do you have any idea how many women I have turned away in the past few years with little or no trouble?"

"Um…a lot?"

He kissed her, twice, brief fierce kisses. "So why am I having so much trouble with you?"

"Mmm. Good chemistry?"

His brow furrowed a little. "It's more than that, Samantha."

Samantha's brow furrowed, too, but way more than a little. "Huh?"

"Never mind." He bent down and brushed his

cheek against hers. "Can you come by the studio on Friday...eight o'clock...street makeup...hair down."

He kissed her between each phrase, slow sexy kisses this time.

Samantha sighed, a sigh of utter bliss. Right now she'd go skinny-dipping in lava if he wanted her to. She didn't even need to ask him what would happen after the shoot. She had a feeling he'd already given her his answer.

"Friday. At eight. Street makeup. Hair down. I'll be there."

SAMANTHA CLOSED *When Amber Burns* and started to toss it on the floor next to her bed as she usually did, then for some reason got up and put it neatly in her magazine rack instead. She couldn't read another word. After Amber's many extra-relationship trysts with studly Adam, Amber was asking herself why she'd gotten involved with Mark in the first place.

Samantha was a trifle irritated with her. Even after the disaster Samantha's marriage with Brendan had become, she could certainly remember why she married him. He was charming, funny, ambitious, elegant, supportive and nondemanding. He seemed to fit her requirements to a T. She just didn't know herself well enough, she'd had so few relationships before, that she didn't know what she needed emotionally.

The bed suddenly annoyed her in its unmade state. She tugged at the sheets, then blankets, then the spread until it was flat and smooth. Plumped the pillows and neatly covered them with the spread. She and Brendan shared values, lifestyle choices—they'd moved in together after the wedding to nearly perfect harmony.

Maybe those didn't turn out to be the right reasons, but it wasn't like she couldn't imagine what she ever saw in him. Amber better get her act together soon because all the hot sex in the world wasn't going to rescue her or the book in Samantha's opinion.

She finished the bed by tossing on the decorative latch work pillow she'd started in high school from a kit her aunt Peg gave her in hopes of inspiring some female activity in her niece, and labored through excruciating boredom to complete, aided by a healthy dose of her mother's nagging.

Passion versus intimacy. Why did it seem so often women had to choose? Swaggering buttheads like Jack who inspired sexual heat, but weren't exactly into unburdening their souls or wanting women to unburden theirs. Or guys like Brendan who saw the world and people, including her, the way they wanted them to instead of how they were. No chance of real intimacy there.

Then guys like…Rick, for example, who even though she hardly knew him, seemed so easy to talk to and happy to share himself and his feelings, who seemed able to zero in on hers with an almost scary intuition, but who didn't exactly inspire her hormones.

She plopped down so hard on the bed, she nearly bounced off it again. So shoot her, she wanted it all.

Not tonight, though. Tonight she needed to go to

see Jack with her head on straight. She needed to get rid of this confusion, this uncertainty, this tendency to analyze and mull and mope, and get clear on what she and he were about.

Her cell phone rang and she groaned and let her voice mail get it. Easy to say change her attitude, harder to do. Jack's little comment about this being more than chemistry had only complicated the issue. She needed it simple. Needed to focus on how this was her Man To Do adventure and leave all the rest alone.

She punched her fist into the boring latch work pillow and dug her phone out of her briefcase which she'd flung on her bed after work today to see who had called. The computer voice came on announcing one message. "Johnny. It's Kimmy. Eight o'clock. Kelsey's. I'll be at the bar with no panties on. You are to come up behind me and touch my ass so I know you're there. Then go to the bathroom in the back by the kitchen. Wait twenty seconds and take off your pants. I'll knock four times. Ten minutes and you'll forget any other woman exists."

Samantha rolled her eyes, deleted the message and punched off her cell phone. Sex in a bar bathroom? Ew. There just wasn't enough disinfectant in the universe to make her want to do that.

She wriggled off her bed, stooped to pick up a magazine and her slippers, tossed there last night just before sleep.

But...

Maybe that was exactly what she needed to hear.

This little rebellious part of her, like a praying mantis waiting to spring out and catch hold of a mate, to use and then destroy, that fierce, sexual part of her envied the total abandon. The way this Kimmy woman could go after what she wanted with utter confidence. *Ten minutes and you'll forget any other woman exists.*

Samantha needed to get to that mental place for her Man To Do adventure. Ditch her insecurities, her baggage, her vulnerability, even her common sense. Indulge that kind of daring and to hell with the consequences.

She kicked off her work heels and peeled down her panty hose, celebrating their loss after the day spent in sticky August heat. Johnny Orion, sexual powerhouse that he was, had obviously met his match in Kimmy. Funny how the calls to Johnny had become sort of fascinating. It was as if he and his female harem were soap opera characters she was becoming familiar with. How these women got her number didn't even seem to matter. Maybe he had a misprint on his business card. Whatever. He was good for entertainment, and today, on her way to a date with Jack, he was damn good for inspiration.

She finished taking off her clothes and jumped into a cool shower, unable to shake the picture of Kimmy, undoubtedly a blond Amazon, taking such total charge of a sexual situation. She hugged herself, water streaming over her face and body, and laughed out loud, the sound echoing off pink tile. There wasn't a single reason she couldn't do the same thing. In an hour she'd be naked in Jack's studio. Tonight she would become a praying mantis, like Kimmy, let herself loose on her male prey to satisfy her needs, though she'd draw the line at biting his head off afterward. Tonight she'd become a perfect sexual being, Jack's ultimate fantasy and her own.

Tonight she would give even give Johnny O. a run for his money.

JACK LABELED HIS LAST roll of film, put it back into the cabinet and brought out fresh rolls for his shoot with Samantha. Tonight, he was going to take some dynamite pictures. He'd spent the last two days envisioning exactly what he wanted. He was ready and willing and totally fired up. Artistically speaking.

On that other matter he wasn't far behind. After the shoot, he was going to give in to his attraction. How he'd come to that decision he didn't know. In a way, it hadn't been like deciding at all. More like admitting to himself what he'd known all along. He and Samantha were destined to spend some good time between the sheets. He trusted her not to destroy him over it. When she wanted the affair to end, whether that was tomorrow or next week or next season, she'd simply disappear from his life.

A canister of film made a sharp bang on the counter where he put it down too hard. He rubbed his forehead, lips tight, stomach tighter. The woman got to him. He knew hardly anything about her except that she made him boil over with lust, and he was already tense over the inevitable end to something that hadn't even begun.

Go figure.

"Okay, boss. We're done." Maria came back into the main studio space, having just escorted out the last of their temporary staff, and raised her eyebrows at the new film. "What's up for tonight? You didn't have enough punishment today?"

"I'm shooting a model for a new series."

"Aha." Maria folded her arms across her chest. "Her."

Jack flicked his eyes over to her, then back to his business. How the hell did she do that? "What 'her'?"

"Don't play stupid with Maria. Her. The Splinter Woman."

"What makes you think I'm seeing her tonight?"

"You've been a pumped-up clumsy mess all day."

"I have not been a pumped-up clumsy mess." He shot her an annoyed look he knew wouldn't faze her in the slightest. "You are way overestimating this woman's effect on me."

One dark pierced brow lifted. The arms stayed crossed.

Jack dropped a roll of film, then banged his head on the cabinet bending to retrieve it. Jeezus.

"I thought you said she couldn't do the dining table well."

"She couldn't."

"So?"

He gritted his teeth. "I'm doing a new series."

A thick-soled, black, square-toed boot started tapping. Jack suppressed the sudden urge to chuckle. As much as he wanted to bury her alive sometimes, he adored Maria, and this was going to get him nailed but good. He was half looking forward to it.

"A series of nudes."

Laughter exploded out of Maria's mouth. "Nudes!"

"She's perfect for the—"

"Yeah, right."

"Maria. I am an artist." He dropped the film on the counter and took her shoulders, trying for a smug patronizing air, afraid at any second he was going to laugh and blow his cover. "I have a vision for this woman."

"Ha! You have a hard-on for this woman."

He lost the battle with his straight face. "At very least, and I'm being very kind here, this is none of your business."

"Of course it is." Maria reached up, took his face in her hands and gave his cheeks an affectionate smack. "I don't want her to hurt you."

Jack rolled his eyes. "She can't hurt me."

"Baby, she can squash you like a bug. You don't know it now, but you will. I've been with you six years, I know what you went through. I know how strong you are. No woman can pull you out of retirement just because she's a hottie. This is something bigger. Question is, does she know that? Or did you make her think she's just next in line?"

His stomach twisted. "She's not after anything but fun."

Maria frowned and put her hands on her hips. "That's what I was afraid of."

"I'm a big boy, Maria, I can—"

"How can we keep you from splatting like a wet Kleenex on glass?"

Jack turned away, lifted his hands in the air and let them drop. He could talk himself hoarse. Nothing would sway Maria from what she'd already decided. He might as well save himself breath.

"Okay, here's what you gotta do." Maria danced around until she was in front of him again. "You got to treat her right."

"You think I won't?"

"No, you don't understand me. Don't give her what she thinks she wants. Don't give her just sex." Maria beckoned Jack forward, black eyes sparking mischief and mystery; he resigned himself to the drama and leaned down. "Give her you."

"Gift-wrapped?"

"You know what I mean. Slip her your brain as well as the big one."

Jack winced. "Lovely."

"I'm serious. Let her see what's under those killer eyes. She'll fall like a ton of rocks."

He straightened away, pushing back a tiny thrill at the thought. Way too much, way too soon. "You're assuming I want her to fall."

"Not assuming." Maria shook her head emphatically and crossed her arms over her chest. "I know you do."

"I see." Jack imitated the gesture to tease her.

"And how do you know that, when I don't appear to?"

Maria tapped her temple with a multiringed finger. "For the simple reason that I am not an idiot like you are."

"Maria—"

"It's not your fault. You're a man, you can't help it. But mark my words, you'll be in love with this one in a few weeks. It's started already. You can feel that much, can't you?"

He kept his jaw wired shut. Oh no. She wasn't getting that much out of him. His interest in Samantha was strong sexually, and her personality appealed to him so far, but she was coming off a divorce and out to have adventures, to find herself. He wasn't keen on risking his heart as part of her therapy program.

Maria put out her hand. "Twenty-bucks says she's The One."

He gave a strained laugh and shook to seal the bargain. He wasn't generally a betting man, but he wasn't backing down now. "Twenty bucks."

"You laugh, but deep down, in the depths of your soul, you know you are going to lose, even if you won't admit it."

He kept the smile on his face and rolled his eyes as if he was indulging her only to avoid more trouble for himself. But he couldn't explain his agitation, couldn't explain the strength of his attraction. And he sure as hell couldn't explain his instinctive fear of examining either any more closely.

8

SAMANTHA PRESSED THE doorbell at the entrance to Jack's studio building. The hot summery air was softening in the evening; a brief thunderstorm just over, had helped ease the humidity. The sun had reemerged on its way down, its rays catching raindrops hanging from the streetside maples and making them sparkle, like shards of glass among the leaves.

The buzzer sounded; Samantha started and grabbed for the heavy door. Inside, the foyer was cool and still; she took the elevator up to the second floor, excited, anticipating, but calm. She'd expected violent shaking nerves, not this quiet certainty.

The elevator reached his floor; the doors slid open.

Jack stood there, hands on his hips, waiting for her. Her stomach dropped, then rose at the sight of him. His dark hair was still damp from a shower; a renegade lock hung over his forehead and made her want to brush it aside as an excuse to touch him. A white T-shirt with a colorful abstract logo from a New Orleans jazz festival set off the smooth barely tan texture of his skin and tucked into jeans that fit the way jeans were supposed to fit.

He was unbearably sexy.

She stepped forward out of the elevator in her sleeveless sundress and nothing else, confident, collected. This was right. This was the most right thing she'd ever done in her life.

"Hi."

He grinned, a flash of white teeth and welcome. "Hi."

For one bizarre second, even while her pleasure at seeing him made her smile so hard the back of her head was tight, Samantha wanted to cry. A little upwelling of emotion that rose and burst, like a bubble in a mud bath, leaving the surface smooth again.

She shook it off. Think praying mantis. Think of Kimmy and Johnny in the bar bathroom going at it like animals. That's what she was here for.

"Come on in." He gestured toward the studio space and preceded her in. In the corner opposite where they'd been shooting the other night, the bed was set, bottom white sheet pulled tight over a mound in the middle, as if a small hassock had been stuck under it.

"Looks cozy."

"Doesn't it." He turned and walked a few steps backward in front of her. "Would you like some wine to help relax?"

"I'm already relaxed."

"Had some at home?"

"No." She lifted her bare shoulders in a shrug. "I'm just relaxed."

He stopped walking, one side of his mouth twisted up in a devilish smile. "That makes my job easier."

She smiled into his eyes until it got awkward, and gestured down at her dress. "So do I just take it off?"

"Hang on." He strode off to a corner of the studio. Samantha examined the bed, imagining herself naked on it, first alone and then...not.

"Okay." Jack called over from the corner. "Lights going out."

The huge studio went black except for one bright lamp casting eerie shadows across the white bed. In an instant, the studio had been transformed from a large commercial space into a small, intimate bedroom.

She heard Jack's steps coming back; he appeared at the edge of the light, then moved into the circle. "There's a sheet on the chair next to you. Wrap yourself in that. I'll do a few shots of you covered and we'll go from there. If you're more comfortable going into the dressing room, that's fine."

Samantha shook her head. No. She didn't need that. Not tonight.

He busied himself with his camera, his back to her to give her privacy she didn't need or particularly want. Tonight her body was open to him, first as an artist and then as a man. She reached behind her, unzipped her sundress and let it slip off her body, emerging naked into the darkness behind the lamp. She found the sheet on a chair and wrapped it around her, the fabric making soft swishing sounds in the silence. She moved into the light. "Do you want me to take off my necklace?"

He turned, and looked her up and down, his eyes

in business mode, assessing, probably making her a photograph in his mind.

This time she didn't let it bother her. She knew what would come later.

"No. I like it on you." He stepped closer and held out his hand as if to take her arm and draw her over to the bed, but didn't touch her. "I want you lying faceup so you're arched backward over the pillows."

Samantha climbed up onto the bed into the eye-squinting light, and draped herself so the lump hit the small of her back, head down on one side, feet down on the other, her middle arched—a human rainbow. She'd worried the pose would be wildly uncomfortable, but the pillows hit her back in the right place and instead she felt stretched and luxurious. She smiled. Probably nothing would feel wrong tonight.

"Comfortable?" His voice came out of the darkness on her left where he stood behind the camera.

"Yes."

"You look good." He emerged into the circle of white light. "Put your arms up above your head, let them fall back on the mattress. Now cross your wrists."

"Like this?" She moved her arms up. The position thrust her breasts out so her nipples touched the smooth sheet. She could see his face now, watch him study her then reach to change the shape and placement of her arms. His hands were warm, his touch gentle.

"Perfect." He took hold of the sheet covering her. "I'm going to rearrange this."

He moved the fabric off her shoulder, draped it up nearly off one hip so her leg was exposed, touching only the sheet, darn him. Her skin was sensitive and alive under the cool cotton, making her impatient for the warmth of his hands.

He walked back behind the camera, out of her range of vision. The white light bore into her eyes, making tiny pink and blue specks within the brightness. She held her breath. These shots had better go smoothly.

"Turn your head slightly away from me. Good. Now keep your features calm. And Samantha?"

"Yes."

"You can think about sex."

She smiled. "Believe me I am."

The camera clicked.

"Think about it more." His voice was low, soothing, intimate, even echoing slightly in the large room. "Tell me what turns you on."

Samantha's eyes widened. The camera clicked again. She swallowed. *Think Kimmy.* "I...uh..."

"Tell me about the best sex you ever had."

She closed her eyes. *Click.* That was easy. "Right after I graduated from Northwestern. I went to a club one night."

"Lift your left leg just a bit. Yes. Like that. Go on."

"I was all dressed up. I felt sexy and sort of defiant. My college boyfriend had dumped me—my first love—and I was coming out of that pain, but bitter still."

"Go on."

"I saw this guy at the bar." She smiled remembering her first glimpse of him, tough, cocky, handsome as hell, the kind of guy she generally avoided like the plague. The camera clicked. "He was gorgeous, built, a woman's fantasy."

"And you wanted him." His voice came out of the darkness, gentle and encouraging.

"Yes, I wanted him. Usually I let men come up to me. This man I went over to, and bought him a drink. It was the boldest thing I'd ever done. I still can't believe it."

"Why?"

She frowned and stirred. *Click.* "It wasn't like me. It still isn't, not really."

She heard Jack's footsteps coming closer; he appeared in the light.

"I'm going to move the sheet. Are you okay with that?"

"Yes."

He moved the sheet down farther off her left shoulder, exposing her breast. His hand trailed down her waist, pushing the sheet out of the way until the end tangled with her ankles, her left side totally exposed to the camera. The fabric bunched and teased between her legs, a cool smooth bare-weight, like a feathery lover's kiss. Her sex reacted, warming; she had to remind herself to hold still.

Jack went back behind the camera; already she missed his nearness. "Tell me more."

"We talked for a while, then he invited me back to his place."

"You went."

"Yes."

"Tell me what happened."

"We were inside—he had a nice place. He offered me a drink, but I'd had enough. He kissed me and we exploded into this sort of frenzy. He took me into his bedroom and put me on the bed."

"Then?"

"He was the first man that ever went down on me."

"You liked it."

"God, yes." She remembered her ambivalent anticipation, fascination, surprise. *Click.* "I couldn't believe how good it felt."

"Describe it."

"Warm and…wet and…slippery, but really intense stimulation. I was out of my mind."

"Did you come?" His voice had dropped to a low, tense whisper.

"Ohhh, yes."

She heard his sharp intake of breath. "Then what?"

"That excited him." *Click.*

"I can imagine."

"He told me I was the sexiest woman he'd ever seen come."

"God, I can imagine that, too. And then?"

"We had sex."

"What kind?"

"Me on top."

"Had you done that before?"

"Not like this."

"How was it different? Tell me."

"I was really riding him, sitting up straight, up and down with my arms over my head, arching my back." *Click.*

"Like you are now, but upright, riding his cock."

"Yes."

She thought she heard a soft curse come out from behind the camera. This was so damn exciting, separate like this, not even touching, making each other nuts. Her body was begging for him, she could only imagine his was doing the same.

"Did you come again?"

"Yes, I did. He rubbed my clit while I rode him."

Jack came close again, his breathing uneven. He moved the sheet off her other breast, this time allowing his hand to follow so his fingers trailed over her, brushing her nipple; she shivered and arched toward him. "You're making me absolutely crazy, Samantha."

"So are you."

He pushed the sheet down to her waist and leaned over her, kissed her mouth, then her chin, then settled his lips on her throat, making tiny sucking circles with his tongue against her skin. She moaned and wrapped her arms around his shoulders.

"Not yet." He pulled away. "A few more shots."

"This is going to kill me."

"You're telling me." He kissed her once more,

letting his tongue trail over her lips, then disappeared again behind the light, leaving her with a fierce ache between her legs, cursing his control.

"What happened after that?"

She took a second to remember what the heck he was talking about. Her brain was rattled, restructured by the taste and promise of him. Talking about the other guy, whatever the hell his name was, seemed dull in comparison. "We did it doggy style, missionary, the guy was amazing."

Jack chuckled. "We were all amazing in our early twenties."

"That was all."

"Did you see him again?"

"No."

"You must have done all that with other men. What made that the best sex of your life?"

She tipped her head back, considering. *Click.* "For that one night, I was perfect. A perfect sexual fantasy. He didn't have to know I was bitter about men, he didn't have to know that I try too hard to please people or that I tend to change my personality to fit in with whoever I'm with. That I have moments of being overly needy, that I'm totally intolerant of neat freaks and that I refuse to live with anyone who lets the toilet paper feed from the underside. Etcetera."

"Sex without emotion. Without connection. A pure physical act."

"Exactly. And now I have nothing but fond memories of him and he has nothing but fond memories of me. No underlying hatred, no betrayal, no built-up resentment that colors every interaction. It was perfect.''

''And that's what you are looking for with me.''

Samantha swallowed. ''Yes.''

The word came out husky and unconvincing. A restless longing swept through her body and away before she had a chance to study it. ''Yes.'' She said it again, more firmly. That was what she wanted with Jack.

He came back out from behind the camera, walked up next to the bed and bent over her. ''You can't protect yourself against the unexpected.''

She gazed up into his face, his features familiar beyond the brief amount of time they'd spent together. ''I'll take that risk.''

His lips curved into a smile. He backed up two steps and took hold of the edge of the sheet, slid it down slowly and deliberately until her entire body was bared. He drew in his breath sharply, ran his hand down her stomach, pressing his palm over the curling-haired mound of her sex. Her hips rose instinctively; a moan left her throat.

''Jack.''

''Last shots.''

He went back to his camera and she groaned. ''Sadist.''

He chuckled. ''The torture is going both ways here.''

''Good.'' She sure as hell didn't want to be alone in this. ''So what about you? What was the best sex of your life?''

"I haven't had it yet."

She laughed. "Too painful to think it's already behind you?"

"Something like that."

"What will the best sex of your life be like?"

"The best sex of my life will be with the woman I fall in love with."

That strange longing tugged at her for a split second, until she realized he was joking and burst out laughing to show she understood. "Oh, come on."

"I'm serious."

"I thought you weren't a hopeless romantic."

"I wasn't."

Her laughter died. Was this guy for real? She'd never met a man who honestly thought that. They might *say* it; the concept sure sounded good, especially for a woman's ears. But for real? It was such a chick thing to think.

Her brothers had talked about women's worth in terms of their bra size. Her father's ogle-and-flirt approach to every attractive women he encountered hadn't helped. In contrast, Brendan had been practically a feminist in his thinking, but didn't venture at all into the romantic, and all passion faded between them shortly after Samantha's ring went on. She'd been sure Jack fit the brother/father mold.

"What would make that the best sex of your life?"

"Because then sex goes beyond the bodies involved. When the emotional communication is as powerful and erotic as the physical."

Samantha wrinkled her forehead incredulously. He

must be serious. It wasn't like he had to play a Sensitive Male role to seduce her; she'd made it clear what she wanted out of the evening.

"Have you—experienced that with a woman?" She held her breath, irrationally wanting the answer to be no, even as she realized of course it would be yes and who cared? Not like she was in line to give him that experience.

"I've come close, but no."

She turned toward him, brow furrowed, genuinely curious and anxious and a little disoriented. *Click.* "Then how do you know it can be like that?"

"Call it instinct. Turn your body toward me a little, I want to see you."

She lifted her right hip to tip her body toward him.

"Put your left arm under your head."

She obeyed.

"Tell me what you want me to do to you tonight."

Samantha drew her breath in like a tiny gasp. *Click.* "Tell me."

She pressed her lips together. Swallowed. Thought about Kimmy hanging at the bar, naked under her miniskirt, waiting for Johnny to come up and touch her, to signal a beginning of their adventure in the bathroom.

"I want you to touch me everywhere. As if my body belongs to you." *Click.* "I want you to taste me everywhere and I want to taste you. I want to make you crazy with my mouth." *Click.* "Then when you can't stand it anymore I want you to take me hard, and fast, as if I am an object of your lust and nothing more.''

The camera stopped clicking. The air-conditioning went on in the studio space. The light made a creaky cracking sound.

''That's what you want.''

''Yes.''

''Lie back flat again.''

She lay back.

''Spread your legs.''

She spread them.

Jack walked out again from behind the camera and turned off the light. The total darkness made her gasp until the flare of a match lit a tiny circle of Jack's head and right shoulder. The flame moved toward a kerosene lamp she hadn't noticed before, sitting on a nearby table. He lit the lamp and blew out the match. A soft glow illuminated his face. He was watching her, measuring, not moving, just watching.

Then he reached down and lifted the hem of his T-shirt, pulled it up and over his head. She smiled at the sight. He was gorgeous. She knew he would be. Dark, perfectly distributed chest hair, trim muscular build without being overpumped. Yum.

He dropped his jeans and she let out a breath on a silent whistle. Kimmy wasn't the only one without underwear tonight.

''Nice.'' She said the word lightly, teasingly, while her throat thickened. He was so damn perfect. She wanted him intensely. Couldn't wait to get her hands on him, feel his on her. The longing was so fierce it startled her.

"What are you waiting for?" Her voice came out a low hungry whisper.

"I want to look at you. You're so beautiful."

She writhed on the bed, in an agony of emotion she couldn't quite identify. Why wasn't he jumping right in? He was obviously turned-on and ready.

"Please come here."

He moved forward and climbed on the bed beside her, his movements graceful and unselfconscious.

She lay waiting, still arched backward over the pillows, her sex raised up like a sacred offering.

He put his arm around her, moved her gently off the pillows and onto the flat of the bed.

Samantha smiled and drew her hands up the smooth muscles of his arms, waiting for the ecstasy to start.

He bent down and kissed her gently, lingeringly, rubbing his lips over hers, giving brief biting kisses first one lip, then the other.

Samantha responded, part of her holding its breath, waiting for the frenzied assault she'd asked for.

Instead, he continued kissing her, light and teasing. She lifted her head to increase the pressure between their mouths and decrease her frustration. He pulled back, covered her breast with his warm palm and followed it with his head to suck and roll her nipple with his tongue, one then the other. Samantha moaned. She responded to him instantly, powerfully, as if they'd been lovers several times, as if he already knew her body and how she liked to be touched.

He bit her nipple gently; arousal shot down her stomach and landed hot and heavy between her legs. As if he sensed it, his hand followed the same path, over her mound until his fingers spread her labia wide so she felt the cool air of the studio on the moist sensitive place between them.

He moved over her, brushing her breasts and stomach with the coarse hair on his chest, then slid down between her legs. One finger pushed up the skin above her clitoris so the nub was tight and strained. He paused. Samantha's breath came in short pants, loud and anticipating in the silence. His tongue came down on her suddenly, licking hard, sucking alternately. He traced her folds with another finger then pushed hard inside her, one finger, then two, in and out, tracing, pushing, until she felt herself starting to lose control.

She moaned, thrashing her head around, nearly frenzied by the sensations, the always varying pressure of his fingers and tongue. She'd never gotten this hot this fast for any man. She cried his name out, grabbed his hair in both fists and thrust her hips up, pulling his head closer, his mouth closer, the pressure closer, harder, faster until her body took over, the slow certainty and then the bursting, burning wave. She let out a harsh cry, gave over totally to the sensations in her body, selfish, greedy, losing herself completely.

Then came down again. Slowly. Jack's tongue still

probed, gently now, causing shuddering aftershocks. She twisted her head so she could watch him, released her grip on his hair, breath still fast, but slowing.

He kissed the insides of her thighs and lifted his head to grin at her. She smiled back, breathless, sated, happy. He didn't look away. She couldn't either. It was as if they both had something to say, but neither could come up with any words to say it.

Without warning and totally unexpectedly from deep inside her came the horrifying certainty that she was going to cry. Her insides contracted; her throat jammed tight; she clenched her teeth, took a stuttering breath. Oh God, not again. The damn grief was like an evil creature, waiting to pounce when she let down her guard. Not now. Don't. *Don't.* Jack would freak completely.

"I'm going to cry," she managed to whisper.

His smile faded at the contorted miserable expression she could feel on her face. Already he must be wanting to run.

"I'm okay…really."

She barely managed the last syllable before the sobs overwhelmed her. Shit. *Shit.* He must think she was a total basket case. She'd ruined her perfect night, ruined her shot at being his sexual fantasy. Instead, just when it was her turn to satisfy him, to rise up and show her feminine power and glory, she'd become a runny-nosed hiccuping pile of neuroses.

"I'm sorry." She turned into the sheet, feeling an absolute fool, unable to control the outburst. Men had no clue what to do with emotional women. He was probably in the next county by now, at least mentally.

Strong arms circled her, a warm male body slid up behind her. He turned her over in his arms, held her tight to him, his cheek pressed against hers.

Her crying slowed; she struggled to choke the rest back. "I'm sorry. I'm okay now." God he must think her a fright.

He loosened his arms only to change position and gather her tighter. She lay in his embrace alternating between bliss and incredulity. He hadn't freaked. Her crying didn't disgust or appall him. He'd instinctively offered comfort instead of giving into his own reaction, which must have been one of total confusion.

She gave a shuddering sigh and waited for him to release her, to move away, to try and get her back to giving him the orgasm she owed him.

He didn't move. She could feel his heart beating against her chest. Something stirred inside her. Some emotion she tried to identify and couldn't quite, but that grew until it threatened to overwhelm her. She pulled her arms free of his embrace to wrap them around his neck.

For probably five minutes, she lay there with him, drowning in a whirl of emotion: gratitude, shame, bliss, and that strange longing sadness.

Finally he lifted his head. "Okay now?"

"Yes." She met his eyes and the emotion got stronger; she had to look away. "I'm fine. Thank you. I owe you a—"

"Shhh." He laid his fingers on her lips. "There's plenty of time for that. Just relax."

She gazed back up at him with what must be mute adoration. "I think I was—I mean I just—it's that—"

"First time after the divorce?"

"Yes."

He flashed her a grin though his eyes stayed serious. "Hard to keep your guard up during sex."

Samantha narrowed her eyes. "Okay. Tell me now."

"What?"

"What planet are you really from?"

He chuckled. "Been a while since someone held you when you cried?"

She swallowed. Her emotions had horrified Brendan. It had been a hell of a lot longer than Jack could know. "Yes."

He brushed the hair from her face, traced the line of her cheek with his finger. "I'm glad I could do it for you, then."

Samantha stared at him as if he was the first man she'd ever seen. He stared back, his expression changing from quiet and serious to that dark and mischievous and hungry look she could deal with so much better. Relief flowed through her. This had all gotten a hell of a lot more intense than she'd bargained for. The return of the butthead was welcome.

"Now, Samantha." He leaned over and kissed her deeply, rolled his body over her until she was pinned securely beneath his warm weight. "What did you say about owing me one?"

9

From: Samantha Tyler
Sent: Tuesday
To: Erin Thatcher; Tess Norton
Subject: The Eagle Has Landed

I did it! I got some!

Samantha wrinkled her nose at the screen. Erin and Tess would cheer, but talking that way about what happened between Jack and her didn't feel right.

She deleted the line.

So...things went last night, but not quite the way I expected. Let me start this way: Jack is now officially my Man To Do. Or maybe I should say my Man Done.

The sex was amazing. I couldn't believe how good we were together. Maybe it was like that when Brendan and I were starting out, but I don't remember being that responsive to anyone before. Instead of having to work for orgasms (note plural) it was like I couldn't help having them.

It wasn't just his technique either. There was something about the way we connected...

Samantha frowned. Erased that paragraph. More than the girls needed to know. Not what she wanted to dwell on.

His technique was amazing. He knew exactly what buttons to push at what time, so to speak.

One small damper—literally—after my first orgasm I cried my eyes out. And you know what? Instead of freaking out, he held me. And while I was in his arms, I swear, it was the most amazing haven. As if I…

She jerked her fingers off the keyboard and stared at what she'd just typed. *Whoa, Samantha.*

Entire paragraph. Deleted.

The only thing that bothered me was that I came away feeling like he knew a fair bit more about me, some verbal, some instinctive, (you mean there are intuitive men?) but he's still a mystery. Maybe it's just as well. Keeps him enticing in my mind. Familiarity breeds contempt, and all that.

Another thing—you know how people have sex the way they are? I mean you can tell exactly the way someone will be in bed by their personality. Insensitive, selfish, steamroller, bang-all-night-and-think-you're-God's-gift-to-women, or submissive, giving, sensitive, etc., etc.

Jack didn't screw like a Swaggering Butthead. He's kind of confusing. I know I should feel like the conquering Amazon Sex Goddess, but I feel like a junkie who's been given a taste of what she craves. Part of it is just the connection with another human—

we all crave intimacy, no? But I think there's also something more than that, which makes me want to see him again and find out—

Grrrrrr. Samantha erased the last two paragraphs and dropped her hands into her lap. This stream of consciousness typing was going to get her into serious trouble. Jack was her Man To Do. She did him and that was it.

Okay, maybe she'd do him again. A few times. Maybe more. But the divorce book said relationships like this were "transitional" and good for the divorced person as such, preparing him-or-her for when he-or-she was ready for the next real relationship.

Samantha let out a snort of laughter. Why did that sound like a lawyer trying to convince herself of something?

She shook her head and poised her hands over the keyboard again.

Anyway, everything was really good. I don't know if I'll see him again, but he's done a lot already to put me on the road to recovery, so for that I'll always be grateful. That and the multiple orgasms.

Sore and happy,
Samantha

JACK JOGGED UP TO HIS building, stopping to stretch on the sidewalk before he went inside. After going to bed way late, he'd gotten up earlier than usual and gone an extra two miles this morning. This on top of an…active time with Samantha last night and he was still ready to run a marathon.

He put his hands against the trunk of the maple in front of his building and stretched first one calf, then the other, taking deep breaths of the already humid city morning air. A pigeon landed on the cement next to him, then another, pecking and making soft gargling coos. He grinned pityingly at their existence. He wasn't exactly sure what kind of sex pigeons had, but he was damn sure it couldn't touch what he and Samantha had done last night.

They'd lit fires in each other as if they were made for that purpose. She was explosive, responsive, passionate, everything he'd dreamed she would be.

More than that, emotions had burst into his consciousness that he'd forgotten he was capable of. Or maybe he never had been capable of them. Growing up, his parents had been cheery busy people, who dealt with his angst and anger and growing pains by being cheery and busy, volunteering their free time to help people "less fortunate than we are." His problems amounted to nothing compared to what they dealt with every day and he should be grateful for what he had so stop complaining and put a smile on, young man. They weren't equipped to deal with his adolescent rages, or the slide into destructive behavior that started in his teen years and continued until Krista gave him a wake-up call.

So he had stopped complaining, though he didn't bother with the smile, preferring an adolescent sneer. Keeping emotions to himself and acting out became his coping mechanism. After Krista, he'd even stopped acting out. A total automaton until he met Samantha, held her, crying in his arms, and started to feel as if he were coming out of a carefully constructed coma.

Those long incredible minutes holding Samantha had helped him realize that he'd come close to blotting out his life altogether. One night with her, coming off a pure chance encounter in a bar and the instinct that she'd be a natural on film, had done more to animate him than a whole gallon of vodka and an entire agency of models ever could before. And to think he worried that sleeping with her could make him want to go back there.

Not a freaking chance.

He stretched his hamstrings and quads, then walked in a lazy circle to finish his cooldown. The pictures he'd taken last night were even more fantastic than the dining table series. He'd captured her elegance, her reserve and her sensuality exactly as he saw it. She was beyond glamorous, made centerfolds look cheap and trampy. She had a luminous quality about her, maybe it was her eyes, the color of her skin, but she seemed to glow on film. She had the same star quality as women like Marilyn Monroe, or Bette Davis, Sandra Bullock or Julia Roberts. Not just her beauty, it went much deeper than that. His camera had caught the life force in her that made it nearly impossible to look away.

He bounded into his building, took the elevator up and burst into his apartment, shedding his clothes on the way to the shower. Heavy day of shooting in the studio today, he needed to get cracking.

The shower spray hit the tub, he glanced at his sportswatch. Seven-thirty. She was probably awake, maybe already on her way to work.

Fifteen minutes later, dressed in khakis and a polo shirt, he grabbed a bagel out of the toaster where it had been sitting for too long and cooled, smeared it with cream cheese, downed a glass of grapefruit juice and went back into his bedroom to get his shoes.

The pictures of Samantha still lay strewn over his desk where he'd been studying them into the early morning hours. He picked up his favorite: the shot he'd taken of her looking at him questioningly, when she'd asked him how he knew sex with someone he loved would be the best sex of his life.

He could barely understand how he'd been so sure with his answer, it wasn't something he'd thought about much before. But when she'd asked him, a hazy parade of women in various erotic outfits, positions and locations had passed numbingly by. And he suddenly realized that none of that had been good sex. Athletic, sure. Kinky, occasionally. Fun, no question. But faced with a woman who actually made him feel—he'd been certain all that frenzied activity would pale in comparison to what he could have someday. Maybe with her.

His stomach roiled, somewhere between fear and excitement. He couldn't let himself go too much right now, couldn't let himself get too stuck on this woman. She was at a difficult unstable time in her life; she was looking for fun, didn't need heavy stuff, possibly didn't trust her judgment where men and relationships were concerned. If he let on how he felt, she'd bolt. He needed to be patient, give her time to work through what she needed to work through after her divorce. And then...

Jack put the picture down, and picked up his bagel, tore into its tepid chewy texture. And then what? He hadn't a clue. He was new at this. Women hadn't been able to engage his emotions to this degree before, though whether that was a question of timing or a question of Samantha, he couldn't guess. All he knew was that he couldn't stop thinking about her, and that unlike any other woman he'd become fascinated by, thinking about her made him think about the rest of his life instead of just how soon they could plan their next sexcapade.

He turned back to the picture of Samantha. His eyes met hers in the photograph. What was she doing now? Was she just out of the shower? Already at work? He'd better hightail it, himself, to set up his studio downstairs, well in advance of the reps from Stoering Medical Systems showing. Maria might already be there.

He reached and brushed dust off the smooth line of her cheek. Maybe he had time for one call. Just to wish her good morning.

RICK FINISHED HACKING into the server for Samantha's Men To Do loop, read her latest and frowned. Something wasn't right. She'd emerged from Jack's building last night dreamy and withdrawn, almost in a trance. He could swear she'd been crying, and if she hadn't seemed peaceful, he would have burst into the building and flattened the bastard.

Then this morning, this note, which she'd written trying to sound like she'd gotten fabulously laid and had a ball. Yet he could read between the lines and tap into her underlying uncertainty. Something didn't add up.

He went into his kitchen, tweaked the gold taps on his white porcelain sink and filled a watering can. His juniper bonsai and his scarlet geranium looked thirsty; his herb garden needed feeding, too.

He opened the doors to his lakeview balcony and turned back to grab the bag of bread he saved for the birds. They'd get more than just day-old baguette crumbs this morning. A brioche he'd left in the freezer too long, which had succumbed to freezer burn. Damn waste. He had a supply of bread and pastry flown out every month from Mon Pain, an excellent New York bakery—croissant, pain au chocolat, pain au raisin. Nothing that good unless you were in Paris.

Samantha would like Paris, the City of Lovers. He should take her there, maybe next spring, when the eternally gray winter skies gave way to the rebirth of the season.

He puttered among his basil and rosemary plants, fertilizing, pruning, watering.

What would make a woman cry one night, and determined to sound happy and carefree the next morning? Even to close friends?

He put the watering can down with a thud that scattered the wrens and pigeons demolishing his Mon Pain brioche. Only one thing.

If what he was thinking was true, he'd have to move forward faster than he would usually think wise at this juncture. He'd probably have to screw another woman, tedious but necessary, and tell her to call with more explicit instructions for a meeting. Send Samantha flowers with an anonymous card to pique her curiosity. And "bump into" her again soon to stake his own claim. Very soon.

Because he had a horrible suspicion Jack Hunter had touched her heart.

From: Erin Thatcher
Sent: Wednesday
To: Samantha Tyler; Tess Norton
Subject: re: The Eagle Has Landed

Okay, Samantha. Sore is good. Orgasms (plural) is better. Happy is the absolute best. But there's also this little thing about show-and-tell. You're telling me you're happy, but it's definitely not showing up in your note. What's really going on? What aren't you telling us about this guy? You sound a little bit on the down side for a woman in the throes of orgasmic bliss.

I love the idea that you two are so good together physically. That is a huge hurdle we girls have to deal with, finding a guy who not only knows where the buttons are but can actually push them at the exact moment we need them pushed. Exquisite, when it happens. And if it didn't happen with Brendan, well, don't be fooled into thinking this means Jack is anything more than your in-betweener. Please promise me that at least????

And please get back here and tell me more about what's going on.

Love you!
Erin

From: Tess Norton
Sent: Wednesday
To: Samantha Tyler; Erin Thatcher
Subject: re: The Eagle Has Landed

Hmm. First, interesting about multiple orgasms. (Notice how I cut right to the chase.) Because, in my vast amount of worldly wisdom, women don't typically have m. orgs with men unless there is a connection of sorts. Which of course means it makes oodles of sense that you are wanting this connection to deepen. Something is happening here, and it may or may not just be animal sex. Maybe (now don't freak) you LIKE this guy. Maybe you feel there are possibilities. Maybe you can give yourself permission to find out. Just a thought. :)

Remember, sweetie, you deserve all the wonderful things in life, including love, and that just because something is scary doesn't mean it can't be fabulous. Take a chance. Go out on that limb. What if…?

Love and kisses,
Tess

SAMANTHA TRAILED HER fingers over her keyboard. No use. She hadn't gotten a thing done for the last hour. Or two. Jack had called the morning after they'd been together, just to say good morning, just to see how she was, how she was feeling. She'd practically hyperventilated hearing his deep voice on the line. They'd talked only five minutes or so, but it had been friendly and easy. He'd called again the next morning, and this morning, too. *Good morning, Samantha, did you sleep well? What's your day going to be like?*

Just that. Friendly chatter. No word about seeing her again. No flirting, no innuendo. Just like a—she curled her lip—*buddy*.

The problem was, she'd told herself this was what she wanted. Not to be pressured into anything. Just a casual friendly fling, maybe meeting once in a while for sex, maybe not. This restless incessant thinking about him was not part of her Divorce Recovery Plan. She wanted to see him again. She was *dying* to see him again. And not just for his body either. To talk to him, feel that intimate connection. Just to be together, knowing they were lovers.

More than that, she wanted to know about him, wanted him to open up to her, show her parts of himself he obviously was in the habit of keeping hidden. The other night he'd surprised her by showing an intuitive side. He'd read her pretty well, understood why she cried. But shared nothing of himself.

She shoved herself away from the computer. Why beat herself up? The human need for someone to share part of every day, for someone to be special to, was strong. She could forgive herself for being normal. That's all there was to her seeming obsession with Jack. One taste of intimacy and she'd gone a little overboard wanting more, that was it. At this point all her feelings toward him were sheer narcissism—they were everything about how he made her feel about herself and nothing about how she felt about him. She couldn't have serious feelings for someone who held himself back. Been there. Divorced that.

The books all said that after this type of transitional relationship ended, she should get to a point where she was truly okay on her own. Then she could start a real relationship with someone who could offer her romance, passion and all of himself. Someone who really understood her and accepted her, faults and all. Someone she could love back in the exact same way.

In the meantime, she hadn't a clue what to do about Jack and she hated not having a clue. Should she bring up the possibility of a next date if he called again tomorrow? Leave it to him to do the asking? Call *him* and—

Lyssa tapped at the door and came in, looking radiant in a hot pink linen sheath. "Anything you want me to do before Tanya gets here this morning?"

Samantha consulted her file without really seeing it. "No, thanks. I have everything I need."

Lyssa's hot pink linen stayed in Samantha's peripheral vision. She looked up. "Something else?"

"Can I get personal?"

Samantha pushed back her chair and crossed her arms. "Okay."

Lyssa sat. "What's going on with you?"

"What do you mean?"

Lyssa waved her hand in the air. "You've been— distracted and sort of…dreamy the last few days. I wondered if maybe… You know."

Samantha felt a sappy grin tugging at her mouth and grabbed a pen to distract herself. Yes, she knew. "No, I don't know. Spell it out."

"Is there a Mr. Samantha these days?"

Samantha burst out laughing. "A *Mr.* Samantha? I don't think so."

"So this Jack Hunter who calls every morning is no one."

"No one at all." She felt the blush begin at her neck and work its way up her cheeks to display the lie to advantage.

Lyssa rolled her eyes. "No one. Right."

"How are things with you and Bill after the lunch with Brendan?" *Change. Of. Subject.*

"Fabulous!" Lyssa's face lit up as she tactfully jumped on her cue. "Worked like a charm. Bill was so jealous he immediately vetoed the 'date other people' rule and we're back together."

Samantha frowned. "Doesn't that bother you?"

"That we're back together?" Lyssa's sentence

ended in an incredulous squeak. "Why on earth should it?"

"That Bill only wants to be with you after you made him jealous. I mean is that real?"

"Real?" Lyssa held her hands out, palms up, and shrugged. "What isn't real about valuing something more once it's almost taken away. Haven't you ever lost something you took for granted and then realized how much it meant to your life?"

"I guess." Samantha tossed the pen down and leaned back. "Who the hell am I to give advice about love? Look what a mess I made."

"There's always another chance. Even Mr. Jack Hunter who doesn't exist, even though he—"

"Lyssa..."

"Would you look at the time!" Lyssa glanced at her watch and stood up, grinning. "I better go back out to my desk. Tanya should be here any second."

"Show her in when she comes. I'm ready."

Samantha's smile faded after Lyssa left. Her relationship with Bill made Samantha cranky. Maybe it was just that Lyssa was so lovely and sweet and Bill was the center of a universe populated by one. Maybe Samantha was jealous since things with Jack were so uncertain and Lyssa seemed so happy. Maybe Samantha was too suspicious of men and their motives. Maybe it was just Lyssa's unfailing record of dating jerks and the fact that she seemed to be getting in deep with this one.

The door opened and Lyssa ushered Tanya in.

"Hello, Tanya." Samantha stood and smiled. "How are you?"

"I'm fine." Tanya glanced nervously around the office, a picture of fashion inelegance in a too tight, too short red and white striped skirt, white tights and a low-cut tight knit cherry top.

"Have a seat." Samantha gestured to the chair Lyssa had just left, and sat back down herself.

"Thanks." Tanya sashayed over on scarlet heels that could thread a needle, and which would make Samantha's chin hit the pavement within a step and a half.

Samantha opened her file. "I spoke to Rick Grindle about your accusations."

"Hmph." Tanya flung carefully disheveled dark hair behind her, her long nails looking like red jewels against the dark strands. "He probably made me out to be some kind of tramp who was asking for it."

Yes, that's exactly what he did. "He had a different interpretation of the events you told me about, yes." She folded her hands on her desk. "Tanya, I'm going to ask you again, is it possible you misinterpreted what Mr. Grindle was saying?"

"No way." She shook her head emphatically. "No effing way, excuse my French."

"You're sure."

"Look." Tanya leaned forward, heavily shadowed eyes darting to Samantha's face, then away. "I've been hit on by guys of all kinds. From blue-collar guys who like women like me, women who don't try to hide who they are—to guys like him, like Rick, who think they're too sophisticated to talk to someone like me, but when it comes to sex, they'd sure as hell rather fuck me because their hoity-toity women are too damn uptight to be any good in the sack. You know what I mean? A guy like Rick, you wouldn't know it, but he's a total sex hound. I know it. I can practically smell it. And he can't get any the way he wants it from his society chicks, so he goes slumming for people like me."

She fidgeted in her seat. Samantha remembered the huge elegant man, quoting literature, patiently and sensitively discussing Tanya's emotional state without a trace of censure. "I see."

"I've been divorced for a while. I'm not ready to start something new. I've been messed up real bad by guys. I just want to be on my own for a while, you know? I want to do my job well and I want to be left the hell alone, and I sure don't need some high-handed asshole making me out to be a slut just to cover the fact that he's a slimy pervert." She crossed her arms over her ample and enhanced chest, still not quite meeting Samantha's eyes. "So there."

Samantha sighed. The same as the last interview. A torrent of desperate uneasy self-defense. Contrasted with Rick's calm assertions, on the surface it looked bad for Tanya. And yet some instinct, female rather than lawyerly, couldn't entirely dismiss Tanya's story.

"Rick made a pretty convincing case."

Tanya threw her hands up and let them slap down

onto her thighs. "Look, you're a woman. You know what men are like. Why can't you tell what's real?"

Samantha blinked, then swallowed the sudden lump in her throat and reached for her necklace. Damn it, if she cried in front of Trampy Tanya, she'd go home and impale herself on a bottle of gin. Why the hell *couldn't* she tell what was real? Not with Brendan, not with Jack, not with Bill and Lyssa, and not with Tanya and Rick. All the rules she'd grown up with that ran her life in an orderly and predictable way had been suddenly suspended. *Free for all! Come on in, world, and mess with Samantha's head. She needs a little more confusion right now.*

"I can't solve a case on instinct, Tanya. I need information that will stand up to the law." She pulled out papers detailing Rick's version of events, pretty damn sure that at the end of this interview she'd be no closer to the truth than she was now. "Let's go through it all again."

Half an hour later, she escorted Tanya out. The woman had stood firm and clear, all her testimony exactly the same as the last time. Samantha hadn't been able to confuse or get her to slip in the slightest. There was no question now that she absolutely believed Rick had harassed her.

Damn frustrating. She would have to interview more witnesses, other people in the office now, because she had a feeling she could talk to Rick and Tanya for the rest of her life and never get any further.

Samantha sat back down, made more notes in her

file, read a memo and caught up on her e-mail, barely paying attention to the tasks. Her concentration was shot.

"Well, well." Lyssa walked in, carrying a huge bouquet of crimson roses. "And look what just arrived for you, Ms. Samantha. From the man who doesn't exist maybe?"

"Oh!" Samantha's heart started beating triple-time. A second blush heated her face. Jack. He'd sent her roses. Red ones. As if he'd known she was feeling low and needed reassurance. She touched the soft petals. "They're so beautiful!"

"Aren't you going to read the card?"

"Yes." She reached for it, half-buried among the perfect blooms. Maybe he was one of those guys who couldn't use words to say what he wanted. A guy who called with friendly chatter, but showed his feelings with flowers. And if red roses, sign of passionate love, were his feelings, then she'd see him again, and not as a "buddy."

The thought went straight from her brain to race around the rest of her with total abandon. Apparently her emotions hadn't read all the divorce therapy books. She hadn't even opened the card and her entire body was celebrating. "Of course I'll read it."

She opened the card, trying to act casual in front of Lyssa, her spirits singing symphonic choruses at top volume.

I thought these would make you smile on a confusing day. Thinking of you.

10

JACK BROUGHT THE just-delivered containers of food upstairs to his apartment and set two of them in the oven to keep warm as instructed. Spice-rubbed chicken and pasta with asparagus and mushrooms. The fresh fruit tart he put carefully in the refrigerator, next to the cooling bottle of Sauvignon Blanc.

Everything was ready.

He couldn't remember the last time he'd been on a real live date. The kind where you call a girl and invite her out for the sole purpose of furthering your acquaintance.

Only this time, Samantha had called him. She'd sounded curiously excited, not her usual cautious friendliness on the phone each morning, as if something had triggered a change of heart. Maybe he'd ask her about it when she showed, maybe it didn't really matter. Right now he was just glad she'd called. He didn't have to dwell anymore on these confusing feelings, he could do what he wanted most of all—turn off his brain and enjoy her.

He'd spent way too much time on uncharacteristic angst. She was out for a fling; he could give her one. Whatever happened beyond that, happened. Nothing he could control anyway, so why waste time worrying about it?

The operative word from now on was "chill."

The front door buzzer sounded. He headed for the elevator and grinned at his watch. Ms. Punctual Lawyer was right on time again.

She walked into his apartment, radiant and graceful in an eye-matching blue sundress that buttoned up the front, bringing a burst of soft evening air and her own sexy scent with her.

"Hello, Samantha." He leaned in for a quick kiss he couldn't keep from giving her. "You look beautiful, as always."

"Thanks." She smiled into his eyes, her expression at once hopeful and questioning. For some reason, it made him uneasy, as if she was about to ask him for something he couldn't give her.

"Welcome to Jack's Place." He gestured broadly at the view of his living room and kitchen, frowning when he took a good look himself. When had things gotten so untidy? Not like him at all.

"Jack's Place is fabulous." She walked a few steps into the living room, trailed her hand over the new upholstery on the couch, inspected his Ansel Adams photographs and turned to smile at him again.

Again, he reacted with a wary start. Something mysterious, something we've-got-a-secret about that smile. Only if they did have a secret, he had no idea what it was.

"I thought we could take a picnic up to the roof

of the building.'' He gestured toward the ceiling. ''Great view up there of the sunset.''

''Sounds terrific.'' She walked directly toward him and kissed him on the mouth, a long, sexy, lingering kiss that had him gathering her up in his arms to deepen it further.

She pulled back and gave him a coy smile, still tinged with that deeper meaning. ''I thought you said you weren't a romantic.''

Uh. The kiss? Kind of carnal, actually. Maybe she meant the picnic? Picnic on the roof was sort of romantic, he guessed. Though other women he'd taken up there were definitely not brought there for romance. ''Anyone given the right set of circumstances, is capable of anything.''

''True enough.'' She stepped out of his embrace; he resisted the impulse to pull her close again. ''Can I help carry anything?''

''Sure.'' He walked her into the kitchen and frowned at the traces of grime on the stove, at the unloaded dishwasher and sink infested with yesterday's coffee cups. Apparently he'd had a lot on his mind. He hadn't even noticed the place going to pot until he saw it through her eyes. Very unlike him.

''Dinner care of Lucinda Dave's catering.'' He opened the oven and pulled out the foil containers, dropped them on the stove before he burned his fingers, and closed the door with his foot.

''Mmm.'' She sniffed rapturously.

''And dessert.'' He brought out the tart from the

refrigerator, a flaky crust topped with custard and a colorful arrangement of fresh fruit on top.

"I thought *I* was going to be dessert."

"Yes." He turned from packing the dinner into a large canvas bag. "You will be."

She held his gaze, her eyes shining, the tiny flare of her nostrils showing her immediate reaction to his implication. He came very close to cavemanning her into his bedroom right then, but they'd have more fun letting the anticipation build. Good things were worth waiting for.

"One more thing." He went into his room to get his camera and the file with the pictures he'd taken the other night and grimaced at the clutter on his desk. He rummaged through a pile of bills and junk mail, bent to pick up yesterday's socks for the hamper, and finally found the folder behind his bedside table where it must have slipped.

"Here we go." He brought the file back into the kitchen, handed it and a bottle of wine to Samantha and hoisted the canvas bag. "Ready?"

She nodded and followed him into the elevator, up to the rooftop level and out onto the flat asphalt surface, soft from the day of sun, where he'd built a wooden platform years ago, and this morning laid out an old quilt his mother had bought on one of her many garage-sale trips.

"How perfect." Samantha turned toward the sun, already about halfway down the sky to the horizon and raised her arms, inhaling the evening air.

He stopped with the spice-rubbed chicken in his

hands, entranced by the sight of her slender body stretched out, teasing the folds of her dress. She turned back to him, features alight and glowing. He'd never seen her like this. He had to catch it.

The pan of chicken began to cook his fingers. He dropped it onto the quilt and rummaged in his bag, keeping his eyes on her. "Don't move."

Samantha cocked her head. "Why?"

"You're perfect. I want to photograph you just like that."

"As a human? With clothes?" She pretended incredulous surprise, but he sensed her pleasure.

"Yes." He moved around her, put the camera to his eyes, found her in the center. "Turn to me. Raise your arms, like you did before, toward the sun."

She raised her arms. He nodded impatiently. Quick, before the light was gone. "Don't smile, but look happy. Good. Part your lips, just a little. Now drape one arm across the top of your head—bend the top half of your body toward me just a bit. Hold it. Hold it. Good." He took the shot, took it again.

She was like a sun goddess standing with the jagged, layered geometric backdrop of other buildings and rooftops behind her. A wraithlike beautiful being amid lifeless concrete and brick and mortar.

He became totally absorbed, posing her, placing her, taking advantage of the deepening always-changing light, cementing the spirit and buoyancy and light that was Samantha to be his forever on film, just as she was now.

"Jack." Samantha stood, facing away, body

twisted toward him, arms crossed over her head. "I'm
starving."

He put the camera down from his face, glanced at
his watch and nearly swallowed his tongue. A little
over an hour. "God, I'm sorry. I thought we'd taken
up fifteen minutes, max."

She put her arms down, ruefully rubbing her shoulders. "I think it's been five or six hours."

He grinned, got up from his knees and returned to
the blanket. "I get a little intense when I'm working."

"I noticed that." She dropped onto the quilt with
a sigh of relief. "Feed me, Jack."

He opened the wine and poured her a glass, poured
his own and held it up for a toast. "To the most
gorgeous woman in all of Chicago."

"Ohhh." She grinned mischievously and clinked
his glass. "And to the most handsome man on this
rooftop."

"What a compliment." He rolled his eyes and
dished out the tepid chicken and congealed pasta.

"My pleasure." She took a sip of wine and leaned
back on her elbow, hair hanging down behind her, the
picture of contentment. It struck him again how different she was with him tonight, not smoldering with
overt sensuality, not edgy and nervous. But easy and
natural.

They dug into the food, which managed to taste
delicious in spite of being temperature impaired. He
couldn't take his eyes off her, even in the compan-
ionable silence. She caught him watching her and he

grinned a "got-me" grin and came up with a question in case she felt awkward.

"How is your confusing case going?"

"Confusing."

"Still?"

She washed down chilly chicken with a swallow of wine. "Still. Neither side is budging an inch. I've gone over it and over it and over it and I still haven't a clue. I'll have to interview more people to see if I can shed some light."

"What about your instinct?"

"I can't prosecute on instinct."

"My mom used to say you know in your heart what you can't in your brain."

She put her plate down, sat up and curled her legs under her. "When I got married I was sure I'd found someone who loved me for me and that we'd last forever. It turned out he loved me for what he wished I was and the marriage ended. I don't trust my instinct anymore, or my heart. I need facts now. I need proof. I need concrete, analyzable results that will stand up in court."

She spoke quietly and calmly, but the hand not holding her glass was bunched into a fist, and the fading light caught the shadows under her eyes.

Jack put his wine down, pried her glass out of her fingers and took both of her hands. "Samantha."

He knew what he wanted to say. He wanted to tell her to look into her heart, and trust what she found there. Tell her that she just hadn't been listening hard enough to it, that her heart couldn't lie.

But he wasn't built to spout flowery stuff like that. And it wasn't his place to tell her such things, not yet anyway, maybe not ever.

Instead, he looked into her blue eyes, saw the fear and uncertainty, and had to kiss her.

He kissed her over and over, savoring the taste of her, the feel of her, the way their lips met and fit. She was an inventive kisser, a responsive kisser, and he loved that.

He ran his hands down the strong soft lines of her arms, pushed her blond hair slowly behind her shoulders and drew back to look at her. Her eyes were large and serious, her skin lit by the sunset to a rosy glow. His heart turned over in his chest.

"You are so beautiful."

She smiled and rolled her eyes. "You said that already."

"Let me compliment you." He put a finger to her lips. "I want to. You sit there and take it."

Her mouth shook beneath his finger as she laughed. He grinned, feeling high from the wine and Samantha, and kissed her quickly again.

"I want to show you something." He moved away, drawing his finger down her cheek, found the file and handed it to her.

She opened the file while he watched her face for her expression of delight. She'd love them. He'd be willing to bet her ex-husband had never shown her to herself that way.

"Wow." She studied the pictures, eyes wide, but

more in amazement than pleasure. "Look at me. You made me look so…exotic."

"You are exotic. Sexy. The camera loves you."

She studied the sheets a while longer, then put them back into the file and handed it to him. "Those are wonderful. Thanks for showing them to me."

He accepted the folder, stung by her lack of excitement. The next second he chastised himself. Did he expect her to drop to her knees and worship his genius? She liked the pictures and she said so. End of subject.

He tossed the folder behind him and toppled Samantha onto her back, grinning at her squeal of surprise.

"It's time for that dessert you promised me."

Her eyes widened; she looked around. "It's still light. Someone might see."

"Not what we're going to do."

He put his hand to her calf, slid it up under her dress along her firm, smooth thighs, and cupped her sex through her panties, gratified when her breathing changed instantly, when her body tensed and she pushed against his hand. She responded to him as if she was on a sensual simmer all the time and only needed someone to turn the heat up slightly to bring her to a full boil. That kind of sexuality clothed in innocence and sky-blue cotton was his idea of female perfection.

He slipped his hand under her panties, drew his fingers through her wetness to her clitoris and began a light rubbing rhythm. She lay back, gave herself over to the sensations. He rubbed harder.

She opened her eyes, looked toward the sky, her hips pushing, legs opening wide for him.

He felt a hand at his pants, stroking along his cock, then unsnapping, unzipping and reaching inside. He reacted with a groan of pleasure. Her hand knew what it was doing.

They matched rhythms, silent and surreptitious, the breeze blowing over them, to any observers an intimate couple lying together talking.

The thought excited him further. He pushed more insistently against her palm, against her practiced stroking, rubbed her harder.

She turned her head to look at him, lips parted, a flush broken out on her skin. She was close, her movements restless and tinged with desperation.

Her eyes locked with his, her stroke on him accelerated to a pumping demand.

Oh, man.

He lost himself in her eyes and the touch of her fingers, let himself go, spilled into her hand and onto the quilt, at the same time her body shuddered, her gasps crescendoed into a cry.

In the throes of sharing that pulsing ecstasy through their bodies and their eyes, he knew with sudden certainty that he was falling in love with her.

SAMANTHA LAY BACK blissfully and watched Jack slice into the fruit tart. She hadn't had such a fun evening in a long time. Good food, good conversation and dynamite erotic activity. Everything was going as she'd hoped. Her feelings hadn't once spun out of control. She felt relaxed and happy in his presence, not needy and vulnerable.

She was sure he'd sent the flowers, and instead of scaring her, that delighted her. He was honoring her wishes. Taking things slowly. On the surface playing the lighthearted fling guy with the flirty talk and the outlandish sexual pictures that didn't even look like her. Then down below, in a charming and romantic way, sending flowers to let her know he was truly there for her.

What a guy. She could take her time. Get to know him. Enjoy the sex. And eventually, when she was ready, she could take a look at their relationship and her life and see what she wanted.

In the meantime…she accepted a piece of the tart from Jack and looked it over with delight. Strawberries, raspberries, blueberries and slices of peach and kiwi, arranged in beautiful contrasting concentric circles over custard and what looked to be a stick-to-your-thighs crust.

She ate a mouthful and yet another slow, dreamy smile drifted over her face, this time one he hadn't put there. "Oh, yum."

"You look more rapturous now than you did ten minutes ago."

She sent him a look. "Dubious."

He laughed, and the laugh made him look so boyish and free she realized for all his grinning charm, he didn't let himself go like that often.

"What kind of kid were you?"

His eyebrows went up at her question. "Male."

She laughed, but wasn't going to let him off that easily. "Seriously."

"Angry mostly." He ate another bite of his dessert. "What about you?"

"Why were you angry?"

"Oh, I don't know." He gestured with his fork. "I probably thought the world should conform to my every expectation. Like most teenagers."

"How exactly didn't it conform?"

"Exactly?" He gave her a my-aren't-we-nosy look over another huge bite of tart that made her smile but not back down. "I didn't get everything I wanted. Who does?"

"What did you want?" She knew she was close to being obnoxiously persistent and she didn't care. She wanted to know more about Jack than that he was a good listener, a fabulous lover, and had a terrific florist.

"I don't know, Samantha." He put down his plate and sighed. "Let's see. I wanted to be a rock star."

"What did you play?"

"Bad loud music."

"I mean what instrument."

"Guitar."

"Do you still play?"

"No."

"Do you have brothers and sisters?"

"None."

"Just the dog named Samantha."

He chuckled. "Good memory."

"What else did you expect that didn't materialize, Jack?"

For a second, from the signs of internal war visible on his face, she thought he wasn't going to answer.

"Well... Good grades for one. I thought they should just appear because I wanted them to. I'm not sure it occurred to me to work for them. Not until I got into photography anyway."

"What made you do that?" She was relentless. She didn't care. He was talking. She barely dared move in case she bumped him off track.

"I took it as an elective in high school. Got to know the teacher well, got turned on by the subject and pursued it in college. Worked in a couple of studios then opened my own. End of story."

She nodded, though she was thinking, *no, no, the beginning of the story.* "How did—"

"What kind of kid were you?"

She ate another bite and chewed slowly, pretending to consider how to answer, while she was actually wondering if she could push him further to reveal more about himself. She swallowed the bite, glanced at his tense face and decided she'd better not.

"I was a tomboy. Two brothers and a competitive spirit. I grew up determined to prove I was as smart, fast and aggressive as they were."

"And were you?"

"Not really. I actually wanted to take ballet, but I never did."

"Why?"

She shrugged. "Because I'd labeled myself a tomboy and therefore had to be the best, most consistent tomboy I could be."

He chuckled. "Poor little tutu-less Samantha."

"It wasn't that bad." She took the last bite she could manage and put the plate down. "Not like I was going totally against type."

"Why don't you take up ballet now?"

She opened her mouth automatically to say she didn't have time and she was too old, when it hit her that in reality there was absolutely no reason not to. She could even see herself in that tutu, with pink tights and a pink leotard, shiny satin toe shoes with ribbons up her ankles and a little silver tiara on her head. Like she'd desperately wanted to be for Halloween one year and gone as a baseball player instead. "Maybe I will."

The minute the words came out of her mouth she had a ridiculous sense of euphoria, as if she'd busted free of some invisible weight that had been dragging her down.

For no particular reason except that the feeling was wonderful, she burst out laughing.

He cocked his head. "What's so funny?"

"Nothing. It's just that I had never thought about taking it now. As if I considered all my paths chosen, all my opportunities closed. Which is absurd. Thanks for that, Jack."

He shrugged. "Just a simple question."

"With profound impact."

She looked into his eyes until the familiar surge of

emotion became too intense and she looked away, out west at the sunset. Dimming gray-pink clouds hung in the sky, the actual horizon obscured by the cityscape. A plane left a glowing orange contrail across the deepening blue sky overhead.

The evening was perfect. The last rays faded; the air around them grew rapidly dim.

"Samantha."

She turned at the sound of his voice to find him watching her instead of the sunset.

Her heart did a little flip of panic. His eyes were saying "intense" and she wasn't ready to get intense. The whole evening had been perfect mostly because of its utter lack of intensity.

"Yeees?" She made the word playful instead of cautious, not reacting in concert with his mood.

His face changed. He picked a slice of peach off the pie and held it out to her. "More dessert?"

"No, thanks." She smiled her relief, at the same time feeling vaguely cheated. *Geez, Samantha, you can't have it both ways.* "I'm stuffed."

"Not that kind of dessert." He put the peach slice in his mouth and sucked the custard off it, withdrew it from his mouth and slid it in again.

That got her attention. The sight of his lips and tongue working immediately triggered a response between her legs. What was it about this man? He could probably get her hot washing his hands.

He bit a piece off the slice, ran his tongue over his lips to catch the juice, chewed, swallowed. Picked another peach off the pie and held it out. "Your turn."

She moved toward him, knelt in front of him, parted her lips.

Instead of feeding her, he drew the slice across her mouth. The peach was cool, it painted her lips ripe and summery sweet. He took the slice away and she licked them clean.

He put it to her lips again, she opened them this time, drew the slice in, let her tongue and lips play around it, then tipped her head back to let it slide slowly out.

He watched her intently, eyes darkening.

"Lie down."

She lay down; he bent over her, drew the peach over her lips again, unbuttoning her dress with one hand. Her naked breasts came to life, sensitive and full in the soft evening air; he moved her necklace aside with his teeth, painted her nipples with the fruit, round and around in slippery circles, then sucked the juice off, first one, then the other, his mouth warm after the wind-cooled wet, taking his time with his tongue, occasionally giving her a taste of exquisite pain with his teeth.

She moaned and threaded her hands in his hair, as if she would never let him stop. Ever. He was making her crazy. She was hot and ready all over again. How did he do this?

More buttons unbuttoned, more material pushed aside and slipped down, until she lay naked in the vast outdoors, the sounds of the city muted and hushed below them, the light fading slowly to dark.

"Spread your legs."

She spread them, the breeze and the endless space around them teasing her sex, making it highly sensitive. He drew the peach slice across her clitoris, back and forth with gentle pressure, then painted her labia, slid it down over the core of her sex, teasing, pressing, then pulled back, put the slice in his mouth, sucked off her essence and dipped into her again. "You taste so good," he whispered.

"Jack."

He slid the moist fruit across her clit again, set up a light rhythm. She moaned and rocked her hips. The sensation was incredible, but she wanted more than this. She wanted him inside her.

"Jack." She pulled on his arm.

He put the peach to her lips. "Bite."

She bit, tasting the peach and her own juice, mixing into a fruity tangy sweetness. "Make love to me."

He finished the slice and nodded. Shed his clothes.

She waited impatiently, reaching down to stroke herself as the sight of his body emerged into the dim light, naked and hard, then sheathed with a condom and ready for her. She was on fire to feel him thrusting in her, she wanted to make him lose control, pound her until he came in huge shuddering primal contractions.

He lay on top of her, reached to find her and slid home.

She moaned at the feel of him filling her, wrapped

her legs around him, wrapped her arms around him, *come on , Jack, come on.*

He didn't move. She waited, panting, crazy.

He drew out and moved back in. Once. And lay still.

"What are you doing?" She wiggled underneath him, wanting to claw at his back, force him to give her what she wanted, what she needed.

"There's no hurry." He whispered the words in her ear, moved out slowly, moved back in slowly. Did it again. And again.

He was right. They had all night if they wanted. She forced her body to relax. Let go of the desperation. Concentrated on calming the hot desire to climax.

He lifted his head and looked down at her, pushed again, in then out, slowly, barely moving. Then again. He kissed her, lingering, taking his time, accompanying the kisses with more of those maddening slow thrusts.

She relaxed, a bit at a time, until she accepted his rhythm. The urgent need to come dissipated, though the arousal stayed at an impossibly high level.

He thrust. Again. She gave a little gasp each time, expecting to lose control, catch fire again and demand satisfaction, but somehow it was enough, to linger here at this high level of excitement, over and over again to feel him withdraw and come back, withdraw and come back.

She buried her face in his shoulder and closed her eyes. Withdraw. Come back. Over and over. She lost track of time, totally submerged in the sensations of sex and closeness. How long had they been there on the roof, joined together in the soft-aired darkness? Out and back, out and back.

She wrapped her arms around his shoulders, his neck, gripped him, tasted his skin, planted soft kisses along his neck, under his ear. In. And out. In. And out. So slow sometimes it barely seemed he was moving. Except there was the overwhelming knowledge that they were joined, and not just in their bodies, but more than that, more than that. She still gasped at the thrusts, let out soft cries, but her head was full of Jack, of him, of the night and of this time together that she never, ever wanted to stop, and she couldn't tell anymore if the longing came from her body or her heart.

He lifted his head, kissed her again, said her name. She opened her eyes, looked into his, and it came to her with sudden startling clarity, under his slowly moving body, under his tender kisses and his masculine spell, that if she ever woke up days or weeks or months or years from now and found herself deeply in love with Jack, she'd know with perfect hindsight that the process had started right here.

11

THE WAITRESS SAMANTHA had dubbed Witchtress came over, frowning as usual, and banged Samantha's beer on her table. Samantha put down *When Amber Burns* with little regret. The heroine Amber's passionate trysts with macho Adam were beginning to piss Samantha off. So the chemistry was amazing, big deal. Poor Nice Guy Mark had been ditched by now but still hung gamely on, determined to win the trollop back. Maybe Samantha was supposed to be carried away by Adam's muscles and extra-strength penis, but he sort of annoyed her. Didn't Amber know passion would fade? What she needed for the long haul was someone who would listen and understand her, who really knew what kind of woman she was. Sooner or later, even the most intrepid sex goddess had issues that needed talking out.

She put the book back in her bag and took a sip of beer. She liked to come here after work to study files and watch people. Sometimes Lyssa came with her, today Lyssa had another date with the not-so-enticing Bill. Samantha didn't mind. Blue Moon Tavern had a decidedly non-meat-market neighborhood feel, so she never felt like an advertisement for desperate singlehood.

She reached down to her briefcase to get out the file for the Tanya Banyon case and stopped.

Someone had come over to her table. She felt it. The strong sensation of a presence, not quite pleasurable, not quite foreboding.

"Mind if I join you?"

She looked up to see all six foot, several inches of Rick Grindle.

Samantha let go of her briefcase and sat up straight, trying to calm her sudden case of the flusters.

"Rick, what a coincidence."

"I come here fairly frequently."

"So do I." She hadn't seen him here before, but then maybe she just hadn't noticed, though unlikely, given his size. Not the kind of guy you could lose in a crowd.

He stood patiently beside the chair, waiting for permission to sit. Having drinks with someone she was investigating wasn't the most lawyerly conduct, but after interviews with friends and colleagues of his and Tanya's had yielded only additional contradiction and confusion, she could certainly use a little more insight into his case. Beyond that, he was sort of intriguing in an unsettling way that alternately fascinated and repelled her. On a strange reckless impulse, she gave in to the breach of professional etiquette.

"Would you like to join me?" She gestured to the chair across from her and caught the eye of the Witchtress, who adopted a severely put-upon look and started grudgingly in their direction. "Can I buy you a beer?"

"I'll buy since I'm imposing on you." He glanced at her empty glass. "Not beer, though. Have you ever had a sour apple martini?"

She wrinkled her nose. "What's that?"

"Vodka, sour apple schnapps, triple sec and lemon juice."

"Sounds lethal."

"A velvet hammer." He unbuttoned his jacket and adjusted his crimson tie to lie smoothly on his shirt. "Tastes like a Jolly Rancher."

The Witchtress came over and positioned herself to show maximum resentment. "What'll you have."

"Good evening." Rick folded his hands on the table and smiled at her. "I'll have a Tanqueray martini, extra dry, with a twist, please. And for the lady a sour apple martini."

Samantha started to object, not at all sure she wanted that much more alcohol in her system, then stared in total fascination. The Witchtress had started to blush.

Samantha immediately looked over at Rick, but he continued to watch the transformation calmly, his expression one of aloof politeness.

"Okay." The Witchtress actually spoke shyly instead of her usual snarl. "The bartender will have those right out for you."

"Thank you." Rick smiled once more, then turned back to Samantha, who was admittedly still gaping at him.

"How did you do that?"

He looked completely blank. "What?"

"That woman has been rude to me and everyone else I've seen every single time I come in here."

He shrugged, clearly surprised. "I haven't a clue."

For some reason Tanya's words jumped into Samantha's consciousness. *He's a total sex hound. I can practically smell it.*

Samantha frowned. She couldn't smell a thing except a very nice, very subtle, very sexy cologne. She wished she could ask what it was so she could slather it all over Jack and bury her nose in his skin. Just the thought of it—of him—started up a by now familiar ache of longing she was having an increasingly hard time explaining away by quoting divorce books and practicing denial.

Rick turned those unusual gray eyes on her that always made her feel he was boring holes into her brain. "Since we can't talk about business, may I ask you a personal question?"

"Certainly." She smiled, feeling wary. She had to get past the strange effect he had on her and try to figure out what was going on with him. Maybe alcohol would loosen him up and allow some truer nature to emerge—if there was one.

"Do you come here alone often?"

"Sometimes I come with a co-worker. But alone, too, pretty often. Why do you ask?"

"Because young beautiful women are seldom comfortable on their own. You seem totally at ease."

She shrugged, wondering why he knew so much

about women—or thought he did. "I like the wind-down time and I can get work done here."

"So you don't have to take it home and feel your job is taking over your life and leaving you nothing else." He spoke as if he was finishing her sentence.

She tamped down that strange startled feeling she got when he honed onto the thoughts behind her words. "Yes."

"You're smart to keep life and work separate. Keeps you sane."

Samantha snorted. "Something has to."

He made a sudden movement with his head, as if her muttered words caught his attention on a deeper level than he expected.

"Going through a rough patch?" His voice was gentle and sympathetic.

She shrugged. "Kind of, yes."

"I'm sorry."

She braced herself for more questions, but he simply sat there, waiting, and she had the feeling he was willing to listen if she felt like spilling, and respected her privacy if she didn't. What totally blew her mind was that part of her was even considering telling him about her divorce.

"How do you know so much about women?"

He grinned. "Three sisters, six female cousins, three determined aunts, and my dad died when I was six. Learning about women, understanding them, respecting their differences from men was a question of survival."

Samantha laughed, trying not to compare his easy

openness with Jack's closemouthed reticence, and concentrated instead on the concept. He'd studied women. Grown up around them. Claimed to know them. He was obviously sensitive to her emotions and thoughts. Why would a man like that try to force himself where he wasn't wanted? It didn't make sense.

"So there's no man in your life?"

Samantha glanced at him sharply, but his expression showed only polite interest. "Not really. Sort of. I don't know."

Rick removed his jacket, revealing a nearly unwrinkled white shirt covering massive shoulders, and hung it carefully over the back of his chair. "Unusually hot weather, even for August."

"Yes, it has been." She smiled, grateful for his smooth offer of refuge from an awkward moment.

The Witchtress brought their drinks and a bowl of pretzels, which Samantha had never been served in this place.

"Thank you." Rick gave her his full attention for those two brief words and she nodded and walked away beaming.

"Cheers." Samantha lifted her drink.

He followed suit. "Here's to the start of a lifelong friendship. Or a shared drink and never crossing paths again. Or anything in between."

Samantha laughed and toasted him. No doubt he was charming. But a predator? A pervert? She couldn't see it. If it wasn't for Tanya's sincerity and the tiny sense of unease she felt around him, she'd consider the case closed.

She tasted the drink, then smiled. "It is like a Jolly Rancher."

He nodded, obviously pleased and took a large swallow of his martini.

She took another experimental sip and savored it, then another. The liquid was icy cold, the bite of alcohol contrasted pleasantly with the child's candy taste. "I keep expecting it to be too sweet, but then it never is."

"I knew a woman like that."

Samantha's instincts perked up. He'd think her nosy, but if she could get him talking about women in his life, he might slip something useful.

"Who was she?"

"The first great love of my life."

Samantha took another sip, rather unwisely. The drink was already going to her head on top of the beer, and she needed to stay levelheaded. But the stuff tasted so innocent. "Have there been many?"

He shook his head. "Only her."

Samantha cocked an eyebrow. "You said she was the first."

"There will be one more for me."

"How do you know?"

"Because she's out there." He took another gulp of his martini. "I'll know the second I see her."

Samantha nearly spit out her latest mouthful. "You really believe that?"

"Absolutely." He nodded and put the nearly empty drink down, eyes clear, hand steady.

She held his gaze for a few seconds, waiting for

some trace of cynicism or self-consciousness. Nothing. He truly believed that he could spot the love of his life in a glance, while she was such a mess she wouldn't believe it if he bumped into her wearing a sign on his head.

"Do you think it happens that way for everyone?"

"It depends. I am in a clear strong place in my life now. I know who I am, what I want and who I want. When I find her, I will know."

"But, so…" She struggled to form her sentence, fighting the alcoholic glow, trying to figure out if she should even be saying any of this to a relative stranger, but absolutely dying for a confidante. "If you were in a bad place, like recovering from another relationship…"

"I wouldn't be able to trust feelings I had for another person, no."

"Oh." She took another sip. Then another. So she wasn't crazy. Her confusion and hesitation about her feelings for Jack made sense to another person.

"In a vulnerable state following a breakup, it would be way too easy to mistake attraction, lust or infatuation, for love."

Samantha's hand started shaking. She took a healthy swallow of her drink. Without knowing it, he'd just tapped into her deepest darkest fear. The rooftop scene with Jack, in all its power, the emotion she'd felt so deeply, could be a bundle of neuroses and insecurity. Just as the book said.

Even as she thought it, denial rose up. The feelings had seemed so strong, so right. But then really, how much did she know about Jack to inspire that depth of feeling except that he was wildly sexy and held her when she cried? What could she really love about him other than how he made her feel? "Yes. I imagine."

"Before I came to work at Eisemann, Inc., here in Chicago, I was living in L.A. That was seven years ago. I had been dating this woman for eight years before that. When she left me, I knew I had to change my life completely, that if I stayed there, surrounded by memories of her, I'd lose my mind."

Samantha sipped her drink. Her confusion grew along with her unsteadiness. On the one hand, she felt deep instinctive sympathy. On the other...why was he telling her all this?

She put her drink down in the center of her coaster. "I just went through something like that."

"I'm sorry." He waited, then when she didn't speak, signaled to the Witchtress for another martini. Samantha stared at his empty glass. If she'd drunk that much booze that fast she'd be in the bathroom, head down over the commode. But then she wasn't a human mountain.

"Would you like another?"

"No, thanks, I'm fine." She took another swallow, knowing she shouldn't have any more, knowing she was drinking the seductively delicious stuff way too fast, but already past caring. "So your...change of scenery helped you get over this woman?"

"Yes. I have rebuilt my life, suffered through the lonely times. I'm finally ready to find someone now."

"How long has it been?"

"Seven years."

"Right, you said that already." Samantha put her drink down again, this time nearly upsetting the glass and fiddled with her necklace. "It took you that long to feel stable."

He brought his gaze up from her throat and nodded. "It was that long before I could trust my feelings again. To separate out attraction and infatuation, to understand that I was truly ready. I'm sure it isn't that long for most people. But that's how long it took me. That's how deeply I loved this woman."

"Oh." Sympathy slogged through Samantha's sluggish brain. "You poor man."

He leaned closer, across the table, as if to whisper, his light eyes earnest, almost glowing. "I tell my recently divorced sister this all the time. Please be careful. Don't mistake sexual attraction for love. Hold out for someone who will share himself with you. Who knows who you really are."

She stared into his mesmerizing gray eyes across the table, her breath coming fast and high. *Oh my God.* He was doing it again. It was almost creepy. As if he was reading her mind. Was this how Tanya felt violated? Samantha felt that way now, panicked and paranoid.

"What are you doing?" She put her hand to her head, hearing the faint slur in her own words. "Did you know I am divorced? Why are you saying these things to me?"

"I'm sorry." His face was instantly contrite; he

leaned back in his chair "I didn't make the obvious connection. I was talking about my sister."

Some sense of reality returned. His face was nothing but apologetic. Samantha felt suddenly ridiculous. "I'm sorry. Never mind."

He reached across the table and touched her hand, a warm paternal pat. "It's okay. I've been there. I know how it feels."

She nodded, staring into her glass, feeling too drunk and too stupid and definitely in need of coffee and food before she embarrassed herself further.

The Witchtress arrived with his second drink. He turned to give her a friendly smile. "What is your name?"

"Sally."

"Sally, could you tell me what the dinner specials are tonight?"

"Sure. There's the—" She blushed and fumbled for her pad. "I can't believe I forgot. I've been saying them all day."

Samantha watched numbly as Sally stumbled through specials she probably could usually recite in her sleep. Part of Samantha wanted more, wanted to talk her feelings out with Rick, to get a grip on them with someone who seemed to understand, who'd been through it and come out on the other side sane, stable and happy. Part of her wanted to escape from this unsettling man, call Jack and beg him to hold her for the rest of her life, make her feel peaceful and connected in a way no one had since she was little and her parents had that power. The rest of her wanted to curl into bed and sleep this damn candy apple drink and the rest of her emotional recovery off.

"Thank you, Sally. Those all sound delicious."

Samantha found herself on the receiving end of Rick's gaze again, and though it did nothing for her sexually, she could see why Sally got flustered. There was an incredibly quiet power to this man, that not many men had, that had nothing to do with his size. Maybe *not* coming onto women made him attractive to them?

Who the hell knew? She finished her martini, feeling distinctly fuddled. She better get something in her stomach. And soon.

"Samantha. Would you like to have dinner with me?"

She barely even reacted to this latest intrusion into her thoughts. Did she want to have dinner with him? She shouldn't drive, hell at this stage, she probably shouldn't even walk. And there was a chance she could get to understand him more. There was a chance she could get to understand *her* more.

He lifted his glass and eyed her dramatically over the rim as if he was about to announce he'd sell no wine before its time.

"When the drink has been too good/Fill your belly full of food./No more wine—water instead/A clean plate will clear your head."

His voice rumbled with a vaguely British accent and his face took on a hint of mischief. Samantha raised an eyebrow. "Some ancient proverb? Another of your favorite authors?"

He grinned. "My Irish grandmother. Apparently Grandad could and did put the booze away with a vengeance. She cross-stitched the poem, framed it and hung it over his workshop so he wouldn't forget to come to dinner."

Samantha chuckled and her mood lifted. He was right. The booze was making her maudlin. She just needed to eat. "Yes, I'll have dinner with you. Thanks, Rick."

In a moment so quick she barely had time to grasp it, some instinct registered in his responding smile the slightest touch of triumph.

12

─────────

From: Samantha Tyler
Sent: Wednesday
To: Erin Thatcher; Tess Norton
Subject: Burn, Baby, Burn

I finished *When Amber Burns* last night. I don't know how others in Eve's Apple will feel or how you guys did, but I am so glad she ended up with Mark! I mean, sex with Adam was swell, but you can't base an entire relationship on sexual satisfaction. Mark loved her, he was sweet and romantic and there for her. She made the right choice.

And, um…on a closely related topic, you are going to laugh at me extremely loudly. I think I'm starting to have feelings for Jack that I shouldn't for a Man To Do.

Stop it! Stop it! I can hear you from here. The thing is, at first I thought there was no way. We are so good in bed together, but he barely talks. I definitely don't need another emotionally bunged-up dude in my life.

But now we talk every day and even though the conversations still aren't incredibly intimate, it's getting better. He talks about himself once in a while and it's not quite like he's about to choke to death every time. Maybe he just needs to be more comfortable with me.

And get this... Starting a week or so ago, flower bouquets and cards and gifts started coming in the mail to work, nearly every day. And what is so totally shivery-cool is that we both know what's going on, but he doesn't ever mention them! I hint around about how romantic he is and he just looks at me and grins. It's totally sexy and amazing! It's like we're having an affair, but not cheating on anyone.

You want to know a stupid secret? I grew up such a tomboy, but I had this intense crush on one kid, Nathan Howard. I used to dream he'd send me secret presents, to show he liked me. But of course I was a tomboy, and boys didn't send secret presents to tomboys. They sent them to the girls with budding breasts and styled hair and little cute dresses with matching shoes. It's as if Jack knows I need that kind of silly female attention. Maybe he took some kind of cue when I told him I'd secretly always wanted to take ballet. Anyway, I'm starting to realize that he's pretty incredible.

I'm thinking a possible reason he is keeping the intimate, romantic stuff underground and not pushing it when we're together, is that he still thinks I just want a fling.

Wait! I DO just want a fling, but I mean...oh God, can I ever stop being confused about my feelings? I'm laughing while I'm typing this, because I think the confusion might finally be clearing. At least as much as it ever will.

I know what you would both tell me to do. Stop being such a chicken and take the risk, right?

I think I might.

Scared but happy,

Samantha

P.S. Those weird calls for Johnny Orion have finally stopped.

"LET'S SEE." LYSSA CAME into Samantha's office where Samantha sat scowling at a letter that wouldn't write itself on her computer screen. ManForce executives were on her about this Rick/Tanya mess and she was dragging her feet. Admitting to the world that she couldn't see clear either to absolving Rick or prosecuting him was utterly galling. "Today we have the small padded envelope addressed to Samantha Tyler in that oh-so-familiar handwriting.

Samantha turned, pushed her hair back and tried not to grab too eagerly. This part of her day had become her favorite, right behind her morning chat with Jack.

For the last week or so, their relationship had been split in two. On the one hand the chats, which she loved. Sharing her day, her moods, problems and her activities with someone was sheer bliss after feeling so alone for so long. And even if Jack didn't contribute a full half of the sharing, he did seem more relaxed around her, and he did seem to understand her and what she was going through.

On the other hand, he'd cast himself in the role of

her secret mysterious admirer, showering her with little whimsical gifts, everything from a tiny scarlet ladybug pin to a beautiful pen, flowers, pick-me-up notes on bad days, thinking-of-you notes on good ones, even a love poem of sorts—or at least a strong affection poem—all the things she had caught herself wanting in their day-to-day interaction.

There was certainly nothing wanting in the sex department. They'd had another rooftop date, making love there, then back at his apartment, first in the elevator, then continuing in the living room and finally ending up in his bed. He'd wanted her to spend the night, but at the time Samantha hadn't felt ready.

Now she was close. The side he'd shown her with the notes and cards really made a difference in how she felt about him, or rather in how she felt about her feelings about him. They'd gone a long way toward putting to rest the fears Rick Grindle had tapped into when they had dinner last week. Now she could understand exactly why she had those strong feelings for Jack. Whereas before, who knew? How could she trust general longing and infatuation? Now she could start to see where Jack and she might fit together well.

She opened the padded envelope, beaming at Lyssa and extracted a small cardboard box.

"Ooh! Looks like jewelry again." Lyssa put her hands on Samantha's desk and leaned over to see. "Open it, open it!"

Samantha opened the lid. Her heart skipped a beat. Nested in the cotton batting was a beautiful necklace in gold's three colors: white, yellow and rose, forming a chain of nesting heart-shaped links. In the middle of the coil rested a tiny card.

"Oh, gosh." Lyssa clasped her hands together under her chin. "It's beautiful."

Samantha lifted the necklace out of the box and watched the surfaces catch the light. Her hand went to the slender simple chain at her throat.

"What does the card say? Am I being too nosy?"

"Way." Samantha grinned, laid the necklace carefully on her desk and opened the card. *"When the time comes, take the leap. I will be there to catch you."*

"Ohhh." Lyssa clutched her heart and pretended to swoon. "You have *so* lucked out with this guy."

Samantha's gaze shot to a sparkle on Lyssa's left hand and all thoughts of Jack's gift exited her brain. *"I've* lucked out. *What* is that boulder doing on your finger!"

Lyssa blushed and laughed. "I wondered when you'd notice."

"How long have you had it?"

"He gave it to me last night."

"Wow." She studied Lyssa's face, feeling wonder and envy and awe all at once. "So this is it."

"Yes." Lyssa's head went up and down in total certainty. "This is it, Samantha. He's the love of my life. I know it."

"But." Samantha gestured wildly. "What about when he broke up with you? What about all the problems you were having?"

"Everyone has problems. At some point you have to look past the problems into your heart, and listen to what it's telling you." Lyssa sat and leaned forward on her knees, twisting the ring around her finger. "He drives me crazy sometimes. He can be very self-centered and immature. But you know what? I'm overly emotional and demanding. Who's perfect? At some point you have to trust that if the love is still so strong after a considerable time, if you've gone through bad patches and come out okay, if you can give each other what you need, then you take that leap of faith like Jack was talking about in the card."

Samantha touched the necklace on her desk. After that dinner with Rick, she'd done a lot of serious thinking. Yes, she could communicate easily with Rick, but their relationship was platonic, professional and it was clear to all parties concerned that it was meant to stay that way. How unfair to compare that to her relationship with Jack. She'd told Jack she just wanted a fling. If *she* didn't give the two of them a chance for more intimacy, how was she ever going to find out if he could provide it? How was she ever going to get to know him well enough to discover what she could provide *him?*

Jack respected her wishes to take things slowly, but the cards and gifts indicated he wanted the relationship to deepen. That he wanted and could sustain intimacy. Her feelings were only growing. Why keep pretending this was only about sex?

This morning they'd agreed to meet tonight for dinner at his apartment. Last time they'd been together, when he'd asked if she wanted to stay the night, it had felt too intimate, too domestic, too soon, and she'd declined. Tonight she would bring her toothbrush and overnight stuff discreetly tucked into a large purse.

Samantha's hands went to the back of her neck. She fumbled with the clasp at first, hands a little shaky, but managed to take off the necklace and replace it with Jack's, the cold weight unfamiliar after so many years wearing Brendan's.

Tonight she'd tell Jack how she felt. And if he asked her to stay in his bed and in his life to see what could happen between them, she'd say yes.

"So you want to know what I think of these pictures you took of your girlfriend?"

Jack looked up warily at Maria from the pages of *Master Photographers,* a collection of the best from the greatest which alternately inspired and discouraged him with its brilliance.

He was trying to think of a new angle for photographing Samantha. He couldn't seem to be able to stop wanting to capture her moods and expressions, her energy and vitality. Sometimes he thought he'd feel that way forever. And sometimes when he thought about forever, he wasn't entirely sure he was thinking about photography.

"That's why I gave them to you, yes."

She chucked the prints on his studio desk and put

her hands to her hips. "From the perspective of you as an artist or as a boyfriend?"

Jack frowned. "I take it there's a difference."

She rolled her eyes and muttered something in Spanish that made Jack glad he didn't speak the language. "Damn right there's a difference."

"Okay." He closed the book on the distorted nudes of André Kertész and crossed his arms over his chest, feeling like a teenager about to get chewed out by his mom for not cleaning his room. "Let's hear it."

"Has she seen these?"

"Not these, no. She saw the table shots and the nudes I did of her."

Maria cocked her pierced brow. "And?"

Jack sighed. "Maria, I have a really good suggestion."

Maria put her hands up in surrender. "Okay, okay. You want me to get to the point."

"Ye-e-es."

She grinned and waggled her finger at him. "I'm guessing she didn't like them. Am I right?"

He answered by pressing his lips together and shifting uncomfortably on the chair.

"I thought so. You know why?"

"I'm pretty sure you're going to tell me."

"You are photographing her like a model."

Jack lifted one eyebrow. "And your point would be…"

"She wants to be photographed like a woman."

"Let me get this straight." Jack closed his eyes

and pinched the bridge of his nose as if he was getting a headache, which, come to think of it, he was. "Her nude body and a picture of her enjoying the sunset are not pictures of her as a woman?"

"You guys getting along? You happy?"

"Sure." He tried to answer casually and with confidence, not expecting the attempt to fool her.

"I knew it. You want to get closer and it's not happening." She nodded triumphantly. "Well I want to win our little bet that she's The One, so I'll give you a hint. These pictures tell you why."

"What are you talking about? The woman is a photographer's wet dream." Jack lifted his hand and let it slap down onto his desk. "This is some of my best work. What the hell does it have to do with our relationship?"

Maria took a step closer and leaned into his face. "Look at them. Look at them hard and then look at her next time you see her. Really look. Like a man looks at a woman."

Jack let out a snort of laughter. Maria had certain really good instincts, he'd grant her that, but she'd gone over the top on this one. "Trust me, Maria, I look at her all the time like a man looks at a—"

"Not sex. That's not what I mean." She crossed her arms over her black T-shirt and regarded him sternly, tapping her foot. "You tell her you love her yet?"

"That's it." Jack got off his stool, took Maria by her shoulders and firmly steered her toward the door.

"End of the day, work is done. You go home, you leave Jack alone to get ready for his date."

She leaned to grab her fanny pack as they went by the reception area. "Okay, okay, but you want this relationship to go somewhere you're going to have to make a move to get it there."

"Right, Maria." He grabbed her umbrella from the stand next to the elevator and shoved it into her hand. "Good night."

She stepped on the elevator, gave him a warm grin and waved. "Good night, Jack. Have good sex if that's what you think you want. But then when you finally admit you want a whole lot more, check out those pictures and get ready to fork over my twenty bucks."

"Good *night*, Maria."

The doors closed on a torrent of mumbled Spanish, undoubtedly describing him in terms more insulting than she could use around him in English.

Jack chuckled and went back to his desk. Picked up the prints Maria had thrown there and studied the pictures of Samantha in the sunset to see if he could figure out what Maria saw—or didn't see—in them.

He couldn't. Maria was either too female for him to comprehend, or she was just full of it. Samantha was nothing but stunning the way he'd portrayed her. He'd shot her in black and white again, but printed her onto warm toned paper so she looked natural, fresh, glowing. And so beautiful it made his heart ache to look at her.

Maria was right that he wanted things to progress. He'd been as patient as he knew how, out of respect for Samantha's wishes to keep things simple, out of the lingering confusion she was in after her divorce. But after the intense emotion they shared whenever they were together, he was getting greedy for more of the life force she brought, more of this revved up version of himself. Greedy to know if it might be possible for him to love in a way he'd come to believe was out of his reach.

He touched the smooth line of her calf where he'd retouched the photograph to remove a small scar. And there was still so much he wanted to know about her. And so much he wanted her to know about him.

She'd changed toward him in the last couple of weeks. She seemed to enjoy their morning talks as much as he did, but lately she'd flirted, seemed coy, talked about how romantic he was—which he took to mean that none of her other boyfriends had called every day or taken the time to be really interested in what she had to say. Guys could be pigs. He knew. He'd been one. What he didn't know was if her changed attitude meant she was just relaxing around him or falling for him the way he already had for her.

He squinted critically at some blown-away strands of hair he must have missed in his touch-up of the photo. He'd try to get those brushed out before he showed the prints to her tonight.

The sliding-wood sound of his desk drawer opening echoed in the large room, silent after Maria's exit.

He picked out a retouching brush, thinking about what his feisty know-it-all studio manager had said. Would things with Samantha go faster if he told her the truth of how he felt about her, or would their relationship grind to a screeching panicked halt?

He dropped the brush and opened another drawer, grabbed the contents of his file marked ''Samantha'' and arranged the prints across his desk. He stared at her, first as a table, then nude in the semidarkness, then feminine and sweet on his roof. Felt the hot ache in his groin, and the hotter one in his chest.

And he knew suddenly without a doubt, exactly what he'd tell her. Even if it cost him twenty dollars and a lifetime habit of emotional safety.

SAMANTHA BURST OUT OF the elevator and launched herself into Jack's arms. Even though they'd seen each other only days ago, and even though they were in touch every day, by phone and through his daily deliveries, it felt like an absolute eternity.

She buried her head in the place that seemed made for it, between his jaw and shoulder, and inhaled the sexy familiar scent of his skin. His arms tightened around her and they stayed like that in the hall of his apartment, swaying slightly, while Samantha's heart felt so full she couldn't tell whether she was going to cry or scream, run laps or collapse in a limp heap.

''I missed you.'' He whispered the words into the top of her head and she lifted her face for a kiss to answer him. God knows she'd missed him, too.

He took his time kissing her, which she loved. The contact could sustain her for weeks, she was sure. No food, no water. Only the warmth and softness, the extraordinary exchange of emotions through their lips.

Except...her body awakened slowly to became jealous of her lips, and the kisses changed, became passionate, open, tinged with desperation.

Samantha pulled back her hips and reached down between them, into his sweatpants. He was hardening, but not all there yet. She loved to touch him like this, to feel the blood lengthening and strengthening his penis, feel the transformation and the corresponding mounting hunger between her own legs.

She dropped to her knees, brought him out of the soft knit material and took him into her mouth, sucking ravenously, in and out, fondling the sacs underneath, alternately gently and with a firmer touch, stopping short of causing him pain. She felt his tension mount, his hand reached to cup the back of her head, his hips thrust in time to the rhythm of her lips.

She twisted her head to look up, saw his face, eyes closed tightly, mouth half-open in a silent groan of ecstasy, a look of ferocious male sexuality.

Then he opened his eyes and looked down. They connected, Samantha with his penis in her mouth and his balls in her hand, kneeling at his feet in subservience, and yet holding such power. She was wild for him.

"Don't move." He pulled gently free, went into

the bedroom and came back a minute later, wearing a condom on his still massive erection. He reached to bring her to her feet, pulled her white shirt off her braless torso, pushed her back against the wall. He knelt, ran his hands quickly down her body, over her breasts, took down her knit Capri pants, took down her panties and thrust his tongue into her sex.

Panting, eager, she stepped out of her clothing and lifted her leg to give him better access. He ran his tongue over and around every part of her until she was sopping wet and desperate for him.

"Jack."

He stood again, moved forward until his hard penis pushed against her. She kept her leg up; he grabbed behind her knee and pressed it against the wall, helping her balance with his other hand on her hip, then he thrust home.

She moaned at his entry, at the animal excitement it generated; he lifted her leg higher, thrust harder into her, over and over until she left herself, clutched his shoulders, his back, heard herself crying out, using language she never used, asking him, begging him, ordering him, give it to her, give it to her.

The eroticism, the arousal became so intense she could barely breathe—her lungs filled and emptied in gasping cries. *Give it to me, give it to me.*

"Oh." The urgency built. Sweat broke out over her body. *"Oh."*

He pushed harder, pumped harder, strong muscles working harder.

"*Jack.*" The wave hit, burned through her, she cried out, held him, squeezed him, nearly choked him. Her body went over the edge, pulsed wildly, over and over. She felt him stiffen, hold back, thrust again, and groan as his own orgasm swept him.

Slowly, Samantha came down. Slowly, she became aware of the world around her. The sweat covering their bodies. The cramping pain in her leg. The pounding of her heart and the gradually slowing of Jack's breathing.

He released her leg; she winced at the change from the unnatural position, winced again when he pulled out of her, but not from pain so much that time as loss.

She looked into his eyes, humbled, awed, almost frightened by the power of what had just happened, then even more awed by the power of standing there, gazing at him, her turn to be unable to come up with words to do justice to the moment, but wanting, needing the connection after what they'd shared.

"Stay there."

He stepped out of one leg of his sweatpants, kicked them up and caught them neatly, then walked back into his bedroom, his slowly diminishing penis with that horrible pink latex dangling from it, his hair a mess from her hands going through it.

He was the most stunning man she'd ever seen.

The toilet flushed, then he came toward her, sweatpants back in place, eyes and stride purposeful, holding his camera. She sighed and opened her mouth to protest. *Click.*

"Jack." She held up her hand. "I look like hell."
Click.

"What do you want me to do?"

"Nothing." *Click.* "Just stand there and look at me."

She laughed. *Click.* "Just stand here?"

"Yes." The camera clicked again.

She shrugged helplessly. "Okay."

"Think about the sex we just had. Think about how you feel about me."

She closed her eyes briefly, then opened them, and thought. The sex? Incredible as usual. If it was just sex, she would still be suspicious about the depth of her feelings. But Jack had been so right when he said a few weeks before that this was more than sex. She hadn't believed him at the time, hadn't dared to. After all, she wasn't ready for love. After all, it hadn't hit her when all the books said it was *supposed* to. And after all, what had she really known about how good they were together except in bed?

She touched the necklace he'd given her. Remembered the flowers he'd sent on a down day, the note he'd written when her boss chewed her out for something that wasn't her fault. And on and on. He'd known exactly how she felt, had provided the support she needed at the time she needed it.

This was a whole lot more than sex.

An electronic beep sounded from the kitchen. Jack stopped taking pictures. "Timer. I have something in the oven."

Samantha nodded, pulled on her panties and Capris and followed him into the kitchen, stood beside him at the stove, reached out to stroke the hard muscles of his back under the worn cotton of his T-shirt, unable to keep herself from touching him. "What are you making?"

"Roasted salmon. My mom used to make it when I was growing up. I called her yesterday for the recipe." He gestured to the recipe scrawled on a piece of paper.

Samantha glanced at it and frowned. That wasn't his handwriting. "You wrote that?"

He turned from the stove and looked at her curiously. "Yeah, why? Is my handwriting that appalling?"

"That's not your handwriting." The words came out absurdly loud in the beige-tiled kitchen.

He cocked his head and looked at her as if she had lost her mind. "It's not?"

Samantha laughed, a slightly hysterical sound. "You wrote this."

"Yes." He looked around the kitchen as if searching for her lost mind. "What is the problem?"

She told herself to calm down. Maybe he disguised his handwriting as part of the prank.

"This." She lifted the necklace, not sure what else to say.

He glanced down at it. "Yeah, I noticed you weren't wearing that other one anymore. It's nice."

"*You* sent this to me."

Jack turned off the oven. "No. I didn't. What is this all about?"

"You sent me cards. You've been sending me notes and cards and presents. To my office. Every day." Her voice rose and began sounding a little panicked. Which wasn't surprising because she was feeling a little panicked.

Jack threw down his oven mitts and put his hands on his hips. "Would you mind making sense, Samantha?"

"You didn't send me anything."

"No, I didn't send you anything. I've been trying my damnedest not to push you. Now who the hell is this guy?"

"I don't know."

A burst of incredulous laughter escaped him. "You don't know?"

Samantha shook her head. She felt like she was either about to scream, throw up or have a tantrum. "This can't be happening."

He shrugged. "I don't know what to say. Some guy has been sending you presents and you decided not to mention it?"

"I thought it was you. I thought it was our secret." She grabbed her head in both hands. "The whole reason I fell for you was because of those notes. This can't be happening."

Jack's face turned dark. "You fell for some guy you don't know because he sent you presents?"

"I thought he was *you*."

"Oh, *I* see." His sarcasm barely registered. "You fell for me and then, oops, it wasn't me."

"Yes." She looked at Jack miserably, thinking of what they'd just shared out there in the hall, thinking of its power and beauty. But without the rest of it, without the real communication, the real nonerotic intimacy, it was just good sex. Jack was her Man To Do. This...other person had completed the picture, given her everything she needed. *He* was the person she'd been wanting to give everything back to.

She covered her mouth with her hand and stared at Jack, feeling the tears coming, totally unable to understand what to feel, what to do, how to sort this out.

"Samantha, are you being stalked?" His voice cracked. His face came out of its scowl to register fear.

"I don't know."

"You don't know who he is. You're sure."

"Yes."

Jack strode over to the phone. "We should call the police."

"No." She practically shouted the word.

Jack turned to her very slowly, his hand on the receiver. "No?"

She shook her head. She couldn't explain. She needed time to think this over, to understand, to try and see who it might be. There had been no hint of a threat from the mystery man. She'd felt comforted, supported, hell she'd even half-fallen in love, thinking he was Jack, that he understood her, knew everything she needed and wanted and craved. That finally, finally someone really knew and accepted who she was. And she'd been confident she could do the same for him when he chose to reveal more of himself.

She couldn't call the police. Not yet.

Jack's eyes narrowed. He took a step toward her. "You aren't protecting him by any chance."

Samantha shook her head. "I need to get out of here, Jack. I need to understand what's going on."

He stared at her. "Samantha, this does not sound good to me."

"I'm sorry," She backed toward the door. "I thought I had you and us all figured out. Now I'm not sure I know you after all."

"You know that's funny." He laughed, a short, bitter, humorless sound. "Because I was just thinking the very same thing about you."

13

RICK TURNED AWAY FROM his home computer after reading Samantha's latest e-mail to her Men To Do girls. She and Jack had a fight last night. She thought the gifts had come from him. Initially Rick found it disturbing that all his efforts had been attributed to someone else. Now he realized he couldn't have planned it better. She fell in love because of the things he'd sent her. She'd realize now, when she found out Johnny Orion and Rick Grindle were one and the same, that she could have it all.

He made one phone call, unbuttoned his shirt and headed for the shower.

She was ready.

JACK STARED AT THE pictures he took of Samantha right after they made love in his hallway yesterday evening. She looked ridiculous. Disheveled. Awkwardly posed. Mouth hanging open. Flaws everywhere.

She was the most beautiful woman he'd ever seen.

Damn it, Maria was right. He'd been photographing her as some kind of fantasy. This woman who needed to be understood and appreciated as she was.

She told him she was looking for a fling. Yet even

when the passion and emotion nearly spiraled out of control between them whenever they were together, that's what he gave her, how he treated her. Impersonal morning chats and sex. Fighting himself still, like the angry adolescent who needed someone else to make him feel he was worth knowing, and who didn't know how to reach out for it. Who continued to suppress himself in adulthood, convincing himself all he wanted was booze and sex.

He of all people should have understood what Samantha wanted. But someone else had gotten there first. Someone else had known what she needed, what she wanted. While he'd fought his deepest instincts, closed himself off from her, he was losing the first woman he'd ever loved. To a stranger.

Not calling her this morning at work as he always did had just about killed him. He should have listened to himself then, too. Called her anyway, let her know he wasn't giving up. What ludicrous irony to be telling her that night on his roof to listen to her heart, when he'd been so good about denying his.

He grabbed the pictures and stood. It wasn't too late. He'd make damn sure it wasn't too late.

The elevator doors were just closing behind him when the phone in the kitchen started to ring.

SAMANTHA SURVEYED THE mess in her house with total dismay. She'd made some progress the preceding weekend. Had managed to clear up and throw away a lot. Now it looked as though a bunch of kids lived there.

Kids who liked to play with paper and magazines and coffee cups and mail and piles of laundry.

She'd gone from confused to clear and back to confused. Yesterday's weirdness with Jack had plunged her back into uncertainty. On the one hand, her feelings for him were certainly strong. But what pushed her over the edge into believing they had something real as a couple—the gifts and thoughtful notes—had turned out to be from someone else. Possibly someone menacing. Who the hell knew so much about her daily thoughts and life? Only people she loved and trusted. Lyssa, the girls, her family. And Jack. Nothing made sense.

Her doorbell rang and she flew to the front window to peer out. A florist truck. Her heart reacted with predictable furious fluttering. Was Jack making a first step toward reconciliation? She'd missed his call like crazy that morning at work, but hadn't called him for the simple reason that she hadn't a clue what to say to him. Not until she figured more out about her feelings. About this whole fiasco.

She moved to the door. Maybe she should put their relationship on hold. She really hadn't wanted to get seriously involved this soon after the divorce. Maybe she needed more time to adjust to being single again.

She opened the door to the smiling greasy-haired delivery guy and accepted the stunning arrangement of pink and white flowers—alstromeria, baby's breath, fern, some kind of daisy. And in the middle a single red rose.

Deliberately ignoring the card in order to be able

to act remotely normal, she thanked him and took the vase inside, put it on her dining table in the midst of the clutter and grabbed the card, barely visible on the far side of the arrangement.

"Oh God." The familiar neat masculine handwriting that she thought was Jack's. *He* was sending things to her house. *He* knew where she lived.

She opened the card.

Flowers for a beautiful lady. With love, Johnny Orion.

Samantha took in a breath so deep she wasn't sure her lungs could hold it all. Then let it out on a horrified gasp. The hair at the back of her neck began to prickle. Her skin felt sensitive and skittery, as if bugs were dancing on it.

Johnny Orion, sex fiend, pervert, predator, shallow manipulative horror, was the reason she thought she'd fallen in love with Jack.

But how the hell did he know so much about her, or know her at all? Or were his notes like horoscopes—written cleverly enough that they could apply to practically anyone on any particular day? She hadn't really paid attention. She'd been so full of Jack while she was reading them, that she'd probably wanted to believe they applied so perfectly to her. Maybe that's all it was. Maybe for all her protestations that it was too soon, she'd simply wanted to fall in love.

Because the idea that a stranger was stalking her, that he knew that much about her dreams and days was too terrifying to bear.

She crossed to the phone. She should call the police. Or Jack. Or both. But was it fair to Jack that she go running to him just because she needed protection? What about what the books said, that she should become independent before she—

Samantha chopped her own thought off dead. To hell with the books. To hell with them. She was scared to death and she needed Jack. If that made her a pathetic clinging individual, then tough shit. When she calmed down from this maybe she'd want to take a closer look at the fact that she immediately turned to him for help above all the people she knew and trusted.

She dialed his number, pacing impatiently while three or four hours seemed to pass between each ring.

After about a week, he answered the phone. The sound of his voice immediately made her want to cry from relief.

"Jack?" She tried to force herself to sound calm. "It's Samantha."

"Samantha. What is it, what's wrong?"

So much for sounding calm. "I'm sorry to bother you, but—"

"To hell with that. Where are you? What happened?"

"I'm home."

"Are you okay?"

"Flowers," she whispered. "They came here. To my *house*."

"Stay there. I'm coming over."

"Jack. No, you don't need to. I—"

"I'm coming over."

He hung up the phone. Samantha replaced her receiver slowly. He'd known she needed him just by the tone of her voice. He hadn't hesitated, even after their last visit had ended badly and they hadn't spoken since. What's more, she called him because deep down she knew she could depend on him in any situation.

She stared again around her living room, and was suddenly beset by a tremendous life-altering urge. To clean.

Ten minutes into a frenzied clutter-ectomy, her doorbell rang. She laughed and raced for the door. How could he get here that fast? He must have broken every speed limit known to man.

She flung open the door and her welcoming smile changed to a startled gasp. "Rick."

"Hello Samantha." He smiled warmly, looking large and attractive in a cotton shirt and linen pants.

"What...what..."

His grin broadened, and for a second, she saw something strange in his eyes. He looked hopeful or vulnerable or something. Had he come to confess? Sometimes the strain of being under investigation did that to people.

"May I come in?"

"Of course." She gestured into her house and followed him in, conscious of how tiny his huge presence made her living room look. "I was just straightening."

His eyes flicked around the less-messy room and landed on the flowers on the table.

He turned to her, with that strange look in his eyes that was starting to make her very uncomfortable. What was he doing here?

"I see you got my flowers, Samantha."

Samantha gaped, every sense disoriented. Her brain worked furiously without coherence, her ears buzzed, her cheeks flushed, the room seemed hot and unfamiliar. "*You're* Johnny Orion?"

"Yes." He stepped forward, took her shoulders and brought her up against his chest. His cologne surrounded her, the scent sexy and alluring, but not on him.

He bent down to kiss her. She pushed against his chest and turned her head. "No, Rick. Johnny. Whatever the hell your name is. You've got this—"

He twisted her head, found her mouth, pressed it under his, massive arms keeping her immobile.

"Samantha." He kissed her forehead, her cheeks, gentle sweet kisses. "I've waited for you so long."

Samantha pushed him with all her panicked strength, which wasn't even enough to make him budge. "Let me go."

To her surprise, he did. And stood watching her, his gray eyes puzzled and wary. "What is it?"

"How did you know so much about me?" She fought to calm her breathing, not sure if she was more angry or frightened, but sure as hell she was both.

"Information is easy to gather if you know how."

The lightbulb went off in her brain. "You hacked

into my computer. You read my e-mail. You invaded my privacy. My life.''

''I wanted to know everything about you, Samantha.'' His took a step toward her, his voice husky and tender. ''So we could be together.''

''So you could use the information to seduce me like all those women you had call me.''

He made a slight movement with his head, the way he did when her comments brought him up short. ''I only gave you what you wanted. I will continue to do so. That's no sin.'' He glanced at her throat and frowned. ''Why aren't you wearing my necklace?''

She scoffed at him. ''Because it wasn't real.''

''Of course it was real.'' He scowled. ''I paid—''

''Was *any* of it real, Rick?'' Her voice came out shrill; she gestured wildly. ''Any of it? The female family? The woman in L.A.? Your divorced sister?''

He shook his head, looking puzzled. ''I don't understand why you are so upset.''

''I'm *upset* because—'' She stopped for a big calming breath. Everything Samantha had liked and trusted about Rick Grindle was an act. Everything about him, about the gifts, about their conversations, about his intuition and their seeming connection, was bull. He was Johnny Orion, he was Tanya's ''total sex hound.'' He wasn't real. *He wasn't real.*

Real was the man she'd just talked to, who heard her voice and knew she needed him, who didn't stop to question, but offered himself right up. Real was the power of what they felt when they were together. The foundation they could build on, to see where it might lead them.

"I'm upset, Rick Grindle, because you are totally full of shit. Tanya is going to have her day in court and the way I feel right now, I'm very tempted to join her and have mine."

The second the words were out of her mouth she knew she had made one enormous, colossal, hell of a mistake. Threatening a man she couldn't best with a sledgehammer moments after wounding his pride with rejection. *Oh, shit.*

Rick's face turned red. His mouth worked; veins popped out in his neck. Samantha took an instinctive step backward just as he lunged for her with speed incredible for such a huge man, and brought her up against his massive body for a second time.

"You are meant for me, Samantha. I have worked on you for *months*. I *always* win. Do you understand? I *always* get the girl."

"I hate to sound like the stereotyped hero arriving in the nick of time, but not this time, and definitely not this girl."

"Jack." Samantha twisted in Rick's grip to see him striding toward them, dark and strong and furiously masculine and God did she love him to death.

He nodded curtly, directed a glance of pure loathing at Rick. "That would be me." He approached them, looking as if he was made of steel, as if he intended to dismember Rick with his bare hands. Even Samantha shrank back; Rick's grip on her slackened. Jack pulled her firmly away, safely behind him, and stood toe-to-toe with the larger man. "And, coming soon to a living room near you..." He made a gesture of welcome to her front door. "The police. So I suggest very strongly that you leave the lady alone. Permanently."

"Police." Rick took a staggering step back. Then another. He looked back and forth from Samantha to Jack, then fixed his gray gaze on Samantha again, eyes haunted and confused, his massive power visibly diminished. "Is this how it is, Samantha? After all this? After all I meant to you?"

Jack turned and drew Samantha to him, wordlessly providing strength, support and love. She returned Rick's stare, suddenly calm and for the first time in weeks, utterly sure. "This is how it is, Rick."

From: Erin Thatcher
Sent: Wednesday
To: Samantha Tyler; Tess Norton
Subject: re: Happy Endings!

You know, Sam. A long time ago you told me Friendship + Sex = Love. Do you remember that? I was whining (say it isn't so!) about not understanding what I was feeling for Sebastian—the confusion, the excitement, the total inability to make it from one day to the next, no, one hour to the next, no, one thought to the next without worrying about this Men To Do thing and how crazy an idea it really was.

Now all I can think about is how crazy I am for Sebastian. (And the man even claims to be a fool for me! Amazing!) Looking back now at all those doubts? I have to shake my head and wonder if you and I and Tess weren't all primed for the relationship we claimed not to be looking for. Does that make sense? Maybe our hormones were all in a row or something, lined up with emotions and biology's ticking clock, ya think? (Though I have to say I'm glad Sebastian and I are in tune about kids... maybe, but not now. Right now we're all about us and I like it that way a WHOLE lot!)

I'm so thrilled for you and Jack. (And for Tess and Dash, too!) And I demand that very very soon we get together. NYC to Chicago to Houston...hmm, maybe meet in Memphis???? When you come down a little from your cloud and think you can spend a weekend away from Jack, we'll do it, okay???

Love both of you! Erin Thatcher-Gallo (I absolutely LOVE signing my name these days! Who'da thunk it!!)

From: Tess Norton
Sent: Wednesday
To: Samantha Tyler; Erin Thatcher
Subject: re: Happy Endings!

Well, I'll be damned. Three for three. Who'd have thunk it? <g> Men To Do...such a noble concept, and yet I can't help but think we hit the jackpot. Three jackpots. We are awesome.

I know you and Jack are going to be blissfully happy. As happy as Erin and Sebastian. As happy as Dash and I are. Good grief, I feel like this is a Hallmark commercial.

All kidding aside, I'm thrilled for you, for all of us. And yes, Erin, I want to do the meeting thing, as soon as possible. Because if we wait too long, then I'll be really huge...

Oh, wait. I didn't tell you guys. ::ahem:: WE'RE PREGNANT! I mean, we're pregnant. hehe surprise!

So...let's meet when I can still button my pants. We'll toast with sparkling cider, and we'll talk and laugh till the sun comes up. I want to hear everything about Jack and Sebastian. Every tiny detail.

I have a couple of friends who are interested in joining Eve's Apple. I'll fill you when next we speak, but right now, my honey is telling me my bath is ready.

I love you guys.

Tess

RICK SWALLOWED THE LAST of his second Tanqueray martini, extra dry with a twist, and surveyed the bar full of chatting people with dull disinterest.

She didn't want him.

He still wasn't sure he'd processed the information. Everything had been going so well. She'd responded to his calculated manipulations exactly as he planned. She'd swooned at the stories of his youth, flushed when he talked of sex. He was certain Johnny Orion had gotten her aroused. But when it came right down to it, she didn't want him.

She didn't want him.

A young blonde, stacked and provocatively dressed

strutted over to his table; automatically he gave her his full attention in the way that always got to women.

"Is this seat taken, handsome?"

Adrenaline started to flow, instincts kicked in. Maybe The King wasn't dead. Maybe The King could rise up and rule again.

"No." He gave her a warm grin. "You're welcome to it."

"Thanks." She hoisted the chair and took it over to a nearby table where she sat with a gang of other twenty-somethings. One of them glanced his way and made a remark that made them all laugh.

Rick clenched his fists, looked down into his empty drink. He was middle-aged. He was alone. He'd made a simple mistake with Tanya and would be prosecuted because of it. Now he'd lost Samantha, his finest prize, to a feebleminded ass like Jack who couldn't give Samantha one-tenth of what he could have given her.

Life sucked.

He looked around for Sally, the waitress. He was going to tie one on tonight. Take a look at his life and figure out what to do. He'd lose his job. His reputation. He could go to jail.

"You need another drink?"

"Yes." He looked up at Sally, couldn't even smile. "Another. Keep them coming."

She frowned at him. "Tough day?"

Despair sat like a hot weight in his chest. "You could say that."

"Where's your lady friend?"

"Not here apparently," he snapped.

"Okay, okay." She took his empty glass. "You don't have to bite my head off."

He watched her walk off, firm ass swaying under the short skirt she wore.

She was cute. He liked her.

She came back almost immediately with his martini, and a bowl of nuts. Stood too close and leaned down to put the drink in front of him, giving him a firm, lacy underwired view. Very nice.

"Here's something to eat. If you're going to drink that much, you should have something in you."

"Sally." He caught her arm, looked up into her face with all the smoldering confident lust he could manage, trying to keep the pleading from his face and tone. "How would you like to have something in *you?*"

He held his breath. If she turned him down it was all over. He'd go home drunk off his ass and blow his brains out with his grandfather's pistol. If she said yes, he'd have one more night of mindless fucking here in Chicago, then he'd skip town in the morning. Start over somewhere else. Try to put Samantha out of his mind the way she'd put herself out of his life.

Sally blushed and his chest felt tight, hot, as if his oxygen had been cut off.

"I get off at midnight. See what you can do about getting me off after that, too."

She threw him a sexy pout and sauntered away.

Rick lifted his glass in a silent toast to the heavens

and drained half of it in one gulp. The King was not dead. Long live The King.

SAMANTHA SNUGGLED NEXT to Jack's warm solid body. She couldn't stop touching him, couldn't get close enough.

After Rick had left, he'd held her as if he'd just saved her from the jaws of a mountain lion. Kissed her over and over, held her some more. And it suddenly occurred to her that Jack had been talking with a lot more than words and she'd been too damn caught up in her books and theories to listen. Too damn caught up in the mockery of flowers and jewelry from a wacko pervert who'd skipped town and would probably never be caught or prosecuted because of it.

"Samantha." His voice was low and sexy in the darkness of her bedroom. "You awake?"

"Yes." She drew her hand over the firm lines of his chest and stomach.

He sat up and turned on the light. "In all the excitement, I forgot to show you something."

"What?" She squinted into the harsh brightness, much preferring the moonlight glowing through the open window.

"Those pictures I took of you."

"Oh. Yes." Samantha sat up unenthusiastically. So far the pictures he'd taken of her all looked bizarre and artificial, and while she appreciated his artistic sense and talent, she didn't really like seeing herself that way.

"I made prints of these." He tossed a pile of shots on the bed and stood watching her as if it mattered a great deal what she thought, which made her even more apprehensive.

She picked the shots up and leafed through them. In the first one, her hair was a mess, her mouth open as if she'd been running a marathon, her eyes glazed and surprised by the flash.

In the second, she had raised a laughing hand to ward off the lens. Her mouth was open midword, her eyes half-closed. In the third she was bending forward, scowling semiseriously, her shoulder stuck out at an odd angle and her breasts looked dangly and pathetic.

She loved them.

"This is me." She raised the pile toward him and smiled all her love at him.

"Samantha." He moved forward, knelt on the bed and waddled toward her, managing to make the penguin movement sexy.

She had it bad, no question.

"Before I met you, I'd been on a pretty bad path. Booze and sex, then the opposite extreme. My life hasn't been a pretty picture. But it's mine and I want to share it with you, if for no other reason than to show you what you've brought to it." He cleared his throat and looked supremely uncomfortable. "I'm not good with poetry, or words, or knowing what kind of jewelry to buy you. But you're the first woman I have ever loved like this, and I want to learn how to make you happy."

"Oh, Jack." Samantha rose onto her knees and threw her arms around his neck. "You do make me happy. I'm so sorry for taking so long to understand how. I'd been in my own head and my own pain and my own neuroses for so long, I'd forgotten how to listen to anything but my friends and my divorce books. *I'm* the one who's sorry."

He pressed her back on the bed, buried his head between her breasts. "So can we move on from all the apologies and get to the good stuff?"

Samantha giggled and wrapped her arms around him, cradling his head over her heart. "You know what I want to do tomorrow?"

"I hope so." He moved his mouth over to her nipple.

She arched into his sucking, felt her body respond instantly, the way it always did as if it was programmed to do so only for him.

"Tomorrow I'm going to burn all my divorce books, clean my entire apartment top to bottom and do the gardening. Then I'm going to go buy that yellow VW Bug I've always wanted and sign up for ballet les—"

He lunged for her mouth, cut off her sentence with a long kiss.

Samantha wrapped her legs around him, her heart swelling with longing and love. Message received and understood. She wasn't going anywhere tomorrow and probably not for a day or two after that.

Jack Hunter might not be the greatest communicator verbally. But he said plenty.

All she had to do was listen with her heart.

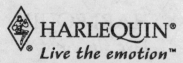

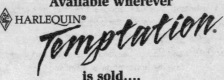
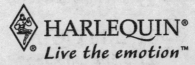

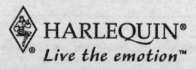

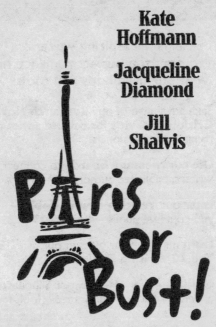